# REDEMPTION
## (THE ROME'S REVOLUTION SAGA: BOOK 3 OF 3)

### BY
### MICHAEL BRACHMAN

# REDEMPTION
## (THE ROME'S REVOLUTION SAGA: BOOK 3)

## Also by Michael Brachman

### The Rome's Revolution Series
Rome's Revolution
The Ark Lords
Rome's Evolution

### The Rome's Revolution Saga
Rebirth: The Rome's Revolution Saga – Book 1
Rebellion: The Rome's Revolution Saga – Book 2
Redemption: The Rome's Revolution Saga – Book 3

### The Vuduri Knights Series
The Milk Run

### The Vuduri Universe Series
The Vuduri Companion
Tales of the Vuduri: Year One
Tales of the Vuduri: Year Two
Tales of the Vuduri: Year Three
Tales of the Vuduri: Year Four
Tales of the Vuduri: Year Five

# Dedication

Each time I publish a new book, my dedications grow larger because the number of people helping me continues to grow. Even so, first, as always, I must thank my brother Bruce. He has always had my back even before I restarted my modern career. Not only is he my editor and artist and the inspiration behind MINIMCOM, but he is also fiercely protective of the Vuduri culture and characters. Bruce creates the amazing covers, the book trailers and makes my writing so much better. Bruce, I could not have done it without you.

My friend Helen has always been a fantastic sounding board. She is quite a spectacular writer and her advice has always been amazing. For this particular book, she taught me about scene and structure and that help me reorganize the chapters into becoming page turners so you would not be able to ever put the book down. Thank you, Helen, for all your support over the years.

I would like to thank Barbara for always encouraging me, reading these books time and time again and helping me to bring humanity to characters that always teetered on the brink of being two-dimensional. Barbara forced me to consider giving all the characters, even the minor ones, some much needed depth so you would care about them as people.

I would like to thank my countless readers for their criticism and suggestions. Sometimes it stung a little but it was always for a good cause.

Finally, my undying gratitude to my wife, Denise, for all her love and support throughout the entire process. She patiently waits while I hide myself in the basement, cranking out what is now over a million words, because she knows I love writing. She even cooperates and allows me to keep my workspace unadorned, despite the fact that it is against her nature, so that my mind can travel to different places and times. Denise, thank you so much and I'll be up around 5:30, I promise. Yeah, right, she says.

# Preface

This story is true. It just hasn't happened yet.

# Chapter 1
## Year 3456 AD (1376 PR)
## Second Planet (Deucado), Tau Ceti System
## (11.9 Light Years from Earth)

NORMALLY, THE PROJECTED IMAGE OF A BLACK BACKGROUND, dotted with stars, would not be much of a reason to panic. But Rome's frantic words were still hanging in Rei's ears.

"Rei, it is happening," she had said. "She cannot get there first. We must go. Now!"

Rome, Rei and their newborn son Aason along with Pegus, the leader of the Vuduri on Deucado, Fridone who was Rome's father, Captain Keller and Melloy, one of the Deucadons, all stood by helplessly, staring at the empty star field.

What they did not see was the small starship that had just made its escape through a PPT tunnel. Its destination was undoubtedly the Earth. The pilot of the fleeing ship was Sussen, a member of the Onsiras, a group whose sole preoccupation was the genocide of the mind-deaf also known as the mandasurte. The Onsiras had fashioned Deucado into a prison world knowing full well that the planet was doomed by an asteroid that was bearing down on them and would exterminate all life twenty years hence.

Rei turned to the image projector sitting on a small table near the window. "MINIMCOM, how long do we have?"

The starship which had once been an autopilot computer named MINIMCOM answered, "Given the type of vehicle hijacked, assuming a sustained velocity of 150c, Sussen will arrive at Earth in 28.96 days but you do not have that much time."

"Why not?"

"She only has to get within distance to connect, not be physically present, to transmit the damaging information."

Rei turned to Rome. "How far out does the Overmind reach?"

"It follows the strength of gravity so it can reach out perhaps a half light year or a bit more," answered his wife.

"So MINIMCOM, what does that translate into?"

"To arrive prior to her connection, you have a maximum window of 21 days."

"Hell, that's not enough time," Rei said in disgust. "How fast can you get us there?"

"`Assuming optimal load, accounting for trajectory…`" The spacecraft/computer trailed off.

"You're stalling," he said angrily, "How long?"

"`4.34 days,`" MINIMCOM answered dramatically. "`I can get there in just over four days.`"

Rome gasped. "MINIMCOM, is this a joke?" she asked. "How is this possible?"

"`It is not a joke,`" replied MINIMCOM matter-of-factly. "`I do not fly the way they do. I now employ a positive feedback cycle to force-project a continuous series of traveling PPT tunnels at hyper-speed. My new skin allows me to stack one tunnel after the other so that the net effect is an uninterrupted tunnel. I can maintain an effective velocity of very close to 1000c for the duration.`"

Everyone held still in stunned silence.

"`There is one small problem, however,`" MINIMCOM added.

"What?" Rome asked.

"`Within my new configuration, there is no real room in my cargo hold for standard living quarters. It would be a very uncomfortable ride and four days is a long time for humans to travel in such discomfort.`"

"What about the Flying House? Could you tow it?" Rei inquired.

"`I could do that,`" MINIMCOM replied. "`However, it would decrease my overall speed.`"

"How much?" Rei asked, irritated.

"`It would roughly double our travel time.`"

"So?" Rei barked, gruffly. "Eight days? We'd still get there way ahead of her. OK, Rome, let's get going," he said.

"Yes," she replied. She looked down at Aason. In her mind, she called out, *"Aason, you are only three days old but we must leave this place. Do you think you will be able to travel?"*

*"Yes, Mother,"* Aason answered. *"I am fine. I would enjoy this."*

"All right," Rome said. "Let us get going."

# Chapter 2

After the group arrived at the small courtyard leading up to the gate, Rei pointed to the flying cart hovering off to the side. "You and Aason wait here," he said to Rome. "I will make sure the Flying House is ready to go. I will come back and get you two in a little while."

"What do you mean two?" Fridone asked. "There are three of us."

Rome turned to look at her father. "No, Beo. It has to be just Rei and Aason and me who travel to Earth. Not you."

"I am not coming?" he asked, his heart catching in his throat. "But my little Rome, I need to be near you. And my new grandson."

"It is not safe yet, Beo. You cannot come and you know why. The Onsiras cannot know that the mandasurte are free here on Deucado yet. Your very presence would give that away."

"No…Rome," Fridone said, his eyes welling up. "I just found you. I cannot lose you again." He stepped next to her, to put his arms around his daughter.

Rome glanced over at Rei. He nodded. "You take all the time you need," he said. "We will be all right." He walked over to a cart, hopped on board and sped off toward the spaceport.

Fridone pushed Rome back to gaze into her eyes. "Rome. Your mother. I want to go home and see your mother. I miss her so much."

"I know you do, Beo," Rome said kindly. "We are going to go to Earth and make it safe for you and all the mandasurte. Then you can come and see Mea."

"But what if something happens to you?" he asked plaintively. "I could not live with the idea of losing you yet again."

"You will not lose me, Beo," she replied sternly. "Remember, MINIMCOM will get us to Earth in just eight days. After we complete our mission, we will be back here before you know it."

"Rome, have you thought about Aason? Who will protect your son while you and Rei are fighting your battle? I would watch him, keep him safe."

"Beo, no," was all Rome said, clearly trying to end the discussion.

Fridone sighed. "You are headstrong," he said. "Unfortunately, you are just like me."

Rome's eyes were glistening too, but she smiled. "Would you expect anything less?"

"I suppose not." Fridone looked away. "Stay here," he said. "Do not leave before I get back."

"Certainly, Beo," she replied, slightly confused.

Fridone reentered the building and was gone for several minutes. When he returned, he had MINIMCOM's conical image projector and two small bags.

"What are in the bags?" Rome asked.

"They are toys. Aason will like them."

*"What are toys?"* Aason asked his mother in her mind.

Fridone set the bags down on the ground. He opened one up and took out a small silver spaceship, glinting in the sun.

In Rome's mind, Aason said excitedly, *"Give me!"* With his tiny hand, he reached out to touch the model starship. *"I like it,"* he said.

"He likes it," Rome said aloud, smiling.

Aason stroked the spaceship. He did not have enough motor control to actually grasp the toy but his fingers scraped it rhythmically.

*"Put it in my mouth,"* Aason said to his mother who reluctantly complied.

While she watched him suck on it, making happy, cooing noises, Keller walked up to Rome. "What exactly are you going to do when you get to Earth?" he asked.

"I know most Vuduri would be horrified if they knew what was happening here," Rome replied. "We just have to get the word out to the population in general. All we need is one Vuduri who we know categorically is not part of the Onsiras."

"That's not much of a plan. How will you know who is and who isn't the enemy?"

"I know one for sure."

"Who?" asked Keller.

Rome looked at her father and took a deep breath. "Mea," she said. "My mother."

"Binoda," Fridone whispered. He bent his head and looked at the ground. His shoulders slumped. Rome rushed over to him and put her hand on his arm. She tried to console him but it was a lost cause.

Pegus gave them a moment before interrupting them. "Rome," he said, "Before you go, the Overmind and I wanted to take this opportunity to thank you for all that you have done here. Thank you for setting us on the right path."

"It was all I could do," Rome replied modestly.

"You were able to convince us which was no small feat. Now it is time for the main event."

"Yes," Rome answered fearlessly.

As she was speaking, the flying cart carrying Rei returned and settled down in its original spot. He hopped out and walked over to his wife and child. "All ready," he said. "The Flying House awaits. They even made us a nursery in the storeroom for Aason."

"That is excellent," Rome replied.

Captain Keller held out his hand. Rome looked to Rei who nodded to her. Rome shifted Aason to her left arm and shook his hand.

"Good luck, Mrs. Bierak," Keller said. "I'm sure you'll do well. I've only known you for a very short time but I think Earth is in big trouble."

Rome bowed her head slightly, smiling the whole time.

"Bierak," Keller said to Rei.

"Yes sir?"

"What are you going to do if you run into one of those Stareater things? Have you thought about that all?"

"Yes we have," Rei answered. "MINIMCOM will shoot some VIRUS units at it and then we'll run like hell."

Keller just shook his head.

*"Mother, what is hell?"* Aason asked Rome.

*"Shhh..."* Rome thought back. "Rei," she said firmly. "Perhaps you could try and remember that we have a child present."

"Oops. Sorry," he said, sheepishly.

Fridone reached over and took Aason from Rome, being careful to cradle his head. "Goodbye, my grandson," he said. "You be a good boy and do not give your mother a hard time," poking Aason ever so gently in the side.

*"I will not, Grandbeo,"* Aason answered silently, laughing to himself.

"He says he will not, Beo," Rome echoed, smiling at the joy she could hear in his mind.

Rome stepped over and into her father's arms. The three of them, Rome, Aason and Fridone hugged for the last time.

"My little Rome," Fridone said quietly, "how you have grown. I never knew you were going to be the one to save the world. I am very proud of you."

"Beo, it is your spirit in me. It is part of you too."

Gently, she pried Aason from her father's arms. Fridone nodded and turned away.

"You take care of my daughter and grandson," he said to Rei. "Do not let anything happen to them."

"That's the plan, sir," Rei said. Fridone nodded.

As Rome was settling into the flying cart, Fridone set down the two bags with toys in them on the rear cargo platform then came back to where Rome was sitting. He rested his hand on her shoulder.

"I love you, Beo," Rome said. Tears were flowing freely down her cheeks.

"I love you, Volhe," replied her father. "Give my love to your mother."

"Of course, Beo," Rome sighed. She turned toward Rei. "Let us go now," she said, "before I change my mind."

Rei saluted the assembly. The cart lifted and began moving along the path that led back to the spaceport. Rome turned back to call out to her father but he was no longer with the group. She surveyed the courtyard and spotted her father running toward Melloy who had just appeared. Fridone was shouting and waving MINIMCOM's image projector over his head. The cart went over a rise and then the compound went out of view.

"Rei," Rome said.

"Yes, honey," Rei replied.

"My father," Rome started. "He…"

"Your father what?"

She shrugged. "Never mind," she said. "I will miss him."

"I'll miss him too. We'll see him again before you know it."

"I certainly hope so," she replied, somewhat pessimistically"

# Chapter 3

AFTER DRESSING IN A PRESSURE SUIT, REI MOVED INTO THE COCKPIT and strapped himself into the pilot's chair. He touched several icons on the viewscreen. The console lit up and Rei was pleased to see that everything was just as he left it. He ran through the preflight checklist with no issues. He cradled the control joysticks and waited for Rome to join him.

*"MINIMCOM,"* he called out in his head. *"Are you ready to go?"*

`"I will be by the time you achieve orbit,"` the computer/spaceship replied via the grille built into the console. `"I am finishing collecting the various items we will need en route."`

"Why are you answering me through the comm link?" Rei asked. "Why not in my head?"

`"This is less distracting. I need you to focus."`

"OK," he said, shrugging it off. "What other items do you need to collect?"

`"I have computed a variety of scenarios for when we arrive on Earth and want to be prepared for all of them."`

"Well, that's good."

Just then, Rome came in through the entryway.

"Aason is settled," she said, placing herself into the co-pilot's chair. "The techs made the nursery airtight. It will be safe even if the cargo compartment becomes depressurized. I did not know how I was going to put him in a pressure suit. Now I do not need to worry. He has promised to be quiet for a while."

"OK," Rei said. "Good. You ready to get this show on the road?"

"Yes, I am," she said, reaching over her shoulder to reach the high-G harness. She started to snap it in place. Rei cleared his throat which made her stop and look at him.

"The last time…" Rei started.

"Do not even say it," Rome answered quickly as she finished securing the harness.

"Say what?"

"I know what you are thinking. Always remember that."

"OK," Rei said laughing.

He looked down at the monitors and ran a perimeter scan via MIDAR. The landing area was clear. He pulled back on the left throttle and the spacecraft lifted smoothly into the air. When they were safely above the structures, he twisted the joystick gently until they rotated around 180 degrees, pointing in the direction of the compound. After they cleared the spaceport, he pulled back hard on the controls and the ship began to ascend swiftly through the atmosphere. When they were high enough, he punched in the plasma drive following the path that MINIMCOM had downloaded until they were safely in a high orbit.

"OK, buddy," Rei said into the grille. "Come and get us."

`"En route."`

"Where are you?" Rome asked. "I do not see you on the MIDAR screen."

`"Behind you and below you."`

Rome widened the range of the screen until the blip representing MINIMCOM encroached upon the scanning circles. The blip rapidly closed in until it was just behind them.

"Do you want me to put this tug in slave mode so you can latch on?" Rei asked.

`"That is not necessary. I am not going to latch onto you."`

"Then how are you going to tow us?"

`"I think transport would be a better word. Please activate the rear cameras. I want to show you my new trick."`

"I will do it," Rome replied and reached forward to press a button on the console. She tapped an icon twice and the viewscreens switched to show part of the planet below them with MINIMCOM's black bulk obscuring most of the star field behind them. Without warning, MINIMCOM disappeared.

"Where'd you go?" Rei asked, perplexed.

`"I am still behind you."`

"No, you're not," he said. He looked down at the MIDAR screen. MINIMCOM's outline was still there. He looked at the viewscreens and all he saw were stars. He looked down at the MIDAR screen. There was no mistaking it. The 3D field of view showed MINIMCOM there plain as day.

"Is that your trick? Messing up the cameras?" Rei asked.

"No, the cameras are unmodified. The image you see displayed is identical to what you would see if you used your eyes."

The hybrid computer/spaceship winked back into view. He was exactly where he was before. Then he disappeared again then he popped back into view again. He disappeared one last time and did not reappear.

"What the he..," Rei stopped speaking. He glanced over at Rome. "What the heck?!" he corrected himself. "What are you doing?"

"It is magic," MINIMCOM said with cybernetic delight.

"MINIMCOM, do not fool around," Rome admonished him sternly. "What are you doing?"

"I took a page out of the book inscribed by the Deucadons. My new skin permits me to project a sphere - froth might be a better word - of PPT tunnels around me. Light and radiation pass through the tunnels from one side to the other. No light reflects so you cannot see me. The tunnels are very short range and I can choose what frequencies pass through them. Unless you knew I was here, you would not know I was here."

"So it's like you're invisible? Sleek!" Rei said admiringly. He looked down at his instruments. "But I can still see you on the MIDAR screen. Your cloak isn't perfect."

As soon as Rei said it, the image on MIDAR screen went blank. Rei glanced over at Rome. She switched the MIDAR off and on again. The instrument was working. There was simply nothing there.

"As I said, I can control what frequencies travel through the tunnels, including those used by MIDAR."

"Buddy, I gotta hand it to you," Rei said, laughing. "You really are a magician."

"Yes," MINIMCOM replied, sounding very self-satisfied. "I have evaluated the situation and have computed that this capability will come in handy when we get to Earth."

"Definitely," Rei said, looking over at Rome. "Now, about the transport?"

"Oh yes," replied MINIMCOM, becoming visible again. "I must come in front of you first."

With series of short bursts of his trim-jets, MINIMCOM ascended like he was on an elevator until he was well above Rei and Rome's tug. He fired his plasma thrusters for a brief moment and used the momentum generated to fly past them. Once he was clear, he used his trim-jets to decrease his forward velocity until it matched that of the Flying House. He lowered himself directly in front of Rei and Rome's tug. The starship opened his cargo door and the ramp lowered and they could see inside MINIMCOM's dimly lit cargo compartment.

"Now what are you going to do? Squeeze us inside there?" Rei laughed.

`"Please take your hands off the controls,"` MINIMCOM requested.

"OK, now what?"

`"Watch."`

With that, MINIMCOM's aft section began to expand. The cavity within changed from a rounded rectangle to triangular, becoming taller and wider. MINIMCOM morphed into a bloated version of himself with his front section obscured by the size of the rear. When the compartment was large enough, MINIMCOM fired his trim-jets gently in retro-mode. Rei and Rome's tug crept forward directly into the cargo hold until MINIMCOM completely enveloped the Flying House. MINIMCOM activated the EG lifters to produce artificial gravity and the Flying House settled gently onto the floor of the expanded cargo compartment.

"He really did, didn't he?" Rei asked in amazement.

"Yes, he did," Rome replied in wide-eyed fascination.

In front of them, they could only see MINIMCOM's interior wall. On their rear view monitors, they saw the cargo door and ramp close and then everything went dark.

"Why am I not surprised?" Rei asked. "Are you airtight?"

`"Yes and no,"` MINIMCOM replied. `"While it would not be difficult to pressurize in this expanded state, it would be simpler to leave it evacuated. You will be safe inside your tug. There is no reason to exit until we get to Earth. I can always pressurize later if there is a need."`

"And your skin, it is basically VIRUS units," Rome asked. "Are you sure it is safe for us to be inside of you?"

`"Yes,"` MINIMCOM replied somewhat hurt. `"I would never, ever endanger either of you. The VIRUS units are completely under my control,"` he said somberly.

"I am sorry," Rome said. "I did not mean to hurt your feelings."

`"It is all right. I do not really have feelings,"` he said, `"just an incredible simulation."`

"Ha," Rei said.

`"Yes, ha,"` replied MINIMCOM. In the background, Rei and Rome could hear the high-pitched whine of MINIMCOM's double set of PPT generators as they came up to full force.

`"It is time to hold on,"` the starship said, `"Next stop: Planet Earth."`

With that, MINIMCOM fired his plasma thrusters and simultaneously projected his positive-feedback traveling PPT tunnel and they were on their way at nearly 500 times the speed of light

# Chapter 4

ESTAR APPROACHED HER TINY APARTMENT DEPRESSED AS ALWAYS. It had been over six months since she and the Tabit crew had returned to Earth. Other than her comprehensive debriefing by the Onsiras when she first arrived home, there had been no subsequent contact with her own kind. She had been commanded to wait for further instructions which up till now had not been forthcoming.

When she first got back, she was instrumental in downloading and analyzing the archives stored aboard the Algol. Currently, she spent her days working in a data center running routine simulations that frankly did not require human attention. The Vuduri and the Overmind of Earth appeared to be looking for a solution to avoid the Stareaters that did not involve VIRUS units but so far no plan had been developed. The pretense of being a good Vuduri was wearing her down.

It was still daylight out when she reached her front door. She opened it, stepped through the doorway and closed the door again. She kept her single high window blacked out so as soon as her door shut, her cramped living quarters were plunged into darkness. She preferred it that way. Less to see meant there were less reminders of the lie she was living every day.

Off to the right, something caught her attention. The lower right hand corner of her workstation viewscreen was ever so faintly lit with a sickly green glow.

Estar's heart skipped a beat but she refused to think about what this turn of events represented because she knew the Overmind was always listening in. Immediately, she began her breathing exercises and mental repetitions to relax and put the Vuduri half of her brain to sleep. Once that portion was deep in a trance, she walked over the workstation and sat down.

She leaned over and caressed the right side of the large flat-panel display, locating a small depression near the bottom. She pressed it three times rapidly. In response, the lower right hand quarter of the screen brightened slightly. In the center of the dimly lit portion, a dull, pulsating green light indicated her secret computer was on and a connection had been established.

"Hello, Estar," the computer said quietly.

"Why are you contacting me?" she directed to the screen, trying to dampen her excitement.

"Reach into your left pocket."

Confused, Estar complied and found a small plastic pouch at the bottom of her pocket. She removed the pouch and placed it on the work surface.

"How did that get there?" she asked.

"The how is unimportant. Within the pouch is a special powder. Mix the powder well with water and make sure you swallow the entire contents."

"Right now?"

"Yes. After you have done so, we will talk."

Estar got up and carried the pouch into the food preparation area. She retrieved a squeezebulb of water and unscrewed the top. She carefully emptied the pouch, which contained a white powder, into the squeezebulb and replaced the top. She shook the bottle well until the powder had dissolved. At that point, she drank all of the water which had a slightly bitter taste. She placed the squeezebulb into the recycler and returned to her workstation.

"I have swallowed it all," she said. "What is it for?"

"MASAL has become impatient with the progression of our species so we have developed a viral antidote for the PPT transceivers that connect an Onsira to the Overmind. Even as we speak, the drug is entering your bloodstream. Once it crosses the blood-brain barrier, it will begin disabling your Vuduri transceivers. Think of the process as a selective form of Cesdiud. When the procedure is complete, you will never be connected to the Overmind again."

"So I will no longer have to use my training?" she asked eagerly.

"No. In fact, once you have been fully transformed, you will be able use your entire brain in service to the Onsiras."

"This is excellent news," Estar exclaimed. She sat back in her chair and a realization hit her. "What am I to do then? I can no longer report to the data center."

"That part of your life is over. We have a new position for you within our main base."

"On Havei?" Estar asked. "How do I get there?"

"There is a transport that has been modified so as to be untraceable. It is located at the coordinates displayed on the screen. Please memorize them."

Some green digits appeared in front of her which Estar stared at until she had them fully committed to memory.

"You are to board that vessel and fly west, over the ocean and across the next continent until you arrive at our base in SoCal. There you are to pick up three more Reonhes who have been similarly prepared. From there, you will proceed west until you reach Havei. Once you arrive at the Big Island, you will receive final instructions as to where to land."

"And then?"

"And then you begin your new life as it was always meant to be."

Estar wiggled around in her seat, barely able to tamp down her exhilaration.

"Am I to go now?" she asked excitedly.

"Wait one hour for the drug to complete its work. At that point your brain should be fully awake. You will find your intelligence level has increased significantly but do not become intoxicated by the result. Maintain your discipline. You must proceed with your mission and do so without being noticed."

"Of course," Estar replied breathlessly.

The screen blanked out.

She got up and walked over to her sofa to await the hour but she was never able to suppress the smile that was spread across her face.

# Chapter 5

MINIMCOM'S NEW MODE OF TRAVEL UTILIZING CONTINUOUS PPT projection was completely vibration-free. The days of stop, start, stop, go were over. The flight was so smooth, there was literally no way for Rei and Rome to even tell they were moving. The continuous emission of gravitic radiation from MINIMCOM's PPT tunnel generators made Rome light-headed but as time wore on, she was able to adjust to it.

After their first full day in flight, they were in the galley, preparing to have an evening meal. Aason was in his chamber, sleeping. On this day, it was Rome's turn to cook so Rei just sat at the table quietly observing her.

"When I first met you, you had longer hair, a lot longer than you do now," he said, finally.

"Yes," Rome replied, running her hands along the sides of her hair, which was just over shoulder length now. She had cut it several inches after Aason was born. "What is your point?"

"Well, all the other Vuduri I ever met, men and women both, they all kept their hair really short," he said. "Why did you have long hair? When you were with the Overmind, I mean."

Rome gathered up the ends of her hair and squeezed them together in a clump. Then she shook her head and it spread out evenly, across the top of her shoulders.

"It was how my mother wore her hair. It was how she raised me. I never felt the need to change it. Vuduri are not slaves to fashion. There was not any compelling need for me to change my hairstyle to match my peers. Perhaps it was my way of protesting certain mistreatments. I cannot say for sure."

"We call that passive aggression," Rei offered.

"Yes, passive aggression," Rome smiled broadly. "Perhaps it was my way of being different."

"But you were a good little Vuduri girl. What gives?"

"You know that I am mosdurece, a half-blood."

"Sure."

"In our society, it is never mentioned or acknowledged, but some treat it as a stigma."

"Yeah, I got that. Vuduri trash," Rei said.

Rome frowned.

"No, no, no," he countered "I don't think that at all, Romey. I'm just saying that was what your buddies thought. We called it prejudice. And I guess it's timeless, huh?"

Rome nodded. "There is more," she said. "On Skyler Base, even though my voice was strong and I was practiced in speaking, that is not why they sent me to interrogate you."

"So why *did* they pick you?"

"They sent me to interview you because of their bias against my mixed heritage. None of the others wanted to be 'soiled' by contact with you. As I told you before, I was the closest thing they had to expendable personnel."

"That sucks," Rei said. He paused for a moment. "Speaking of expendable, whatever happened to that guy who died? The guy whose apartment you gave me."

"He was put into the recycler," Rome said matter-of-factly.

Rei almost choked. "You guys recycle your dead? You don't bury them?"

She turned to him. "We consider it an honor. It is the ultimate sacrifice of an individual for the group."

"But still... Ugh."

"They would have done the same for me if the big, bad Essessoni had killed me," Rome said, playfully.

"Well, I thought about it," he said, smiling. "We Erklirte are pretty bloodthirsty, you know. But you were too cute."

Rome laughed and pursed her lips. Rei just shook his head. A timer went off and she opened the oven. As she turned to bring the food over, she noticed Rei was staring at her but his eyes were unfocused.

"What are you thinking about now?" she asked, setting the food down on the table.

"Huh?" Rei asked, blinking rapidly.

"Where were you? You were somewhere far away."

"I was just thinking back, about the whole thing. About being together." He tilted his head. "Back there, on Deucado, when we first came to the Vuduri compound and they injected you. When you rejoined the Overmind, I, I thought I lost you. And now you're back. I don't want to lose you again. I can't. Romey, I don't think I could take it again."

"Rei," she said tenderly, putting her hand on his. "You will not lose me. Ever. We are doing this so that we can always be together. You already know we were meant to be together. There is nothing in this world that will keep us apart again."

"That's the problem, Rome," Rei said, his voice lowered. "We're not going to be in this world. We're going back to Earth. With the mother of all Overminds. We're taking on a whole planet. A whole race. We're just two people."

Rome bent over and kissed him. "We are two people on the side of right. We will have many friends soon. You will see. And besides, mau emir, we are soulmates. We live inside of each other. We could never really be apart, even if we wanted to."

"No, Rome, you're wrong. I've seen too much," he said.

"I will make it very easy for you," Rome insisted. "Think about this and then tell me the truth, Rei. In the compound, after I was injected, even though I reconnected, think about what you saw and felt. Even though I pretended to not want to be with you, did you really think I was gone? Gone from your life? Is that what your heart told you? If so, why did you even come back for me?"

Rei looked down and replayed the whole episode in his mind again. Attacked by the Vuduri, captured by the Ibbrassati, flying into the Vuduri compound and Rome being reintegrated into the Overmind. His escape and trek through the forest. His sonar-vision, the Deucadons, Captain Keller going on the attack. All to get back to Rome. In a flash, the answer was clear. She was right. Rome was a part of him and he was a part of her.

"I understand! You're right, Romey," Rei said, his face lighting up. "I guess somehow I knew you weren't really gone. You would never leave me. Why did I even think that? What did you do to me? How did I know that?"

Rome leaned forward to touch his forehead then motioned to hers.

"It is the bands, Rei." She looked him in the eye. "I told you. We are our own samanda now and more. We are Asborodi Cimponeti, our spirits are one."

"What about Aason? Is he part of this?"

"Yes and no," Rome said, rubbing her tummy lightly. "You were very kind to never ask me, even once, how it was that I let myself get pregnant."

"Well, you told me that Vuduri women control when they ovulate. So I just figured it was your decision."

"No, it was not my plan," Rome said. "I have been changed. You have changed me, my physiology."

"How?"

"The bands, they are not...read-only, as you say. They are interactive."

"I know that," he said. "I get to live in your memories. I know everything there is to know about you."

"It is more than just knowledge. What happened to us is not their normal function. They have altered our neural pathways. We are...imprinted on each other. We are bound in a way that others never get to experience. It can only be for Asborodi Cimponeti."

Rei sighed. "My beautiful, sweet Rome. You're right. It doesn't matter where we go. We could never be truly apart."

"That is why I say we are our own samanda. And I can now see that a baby is the natural next step. It was nothing I could control nor would I want to."

As she said it, Rome sat down on his lap facing him, straddling his legs. She kissed him deeply. She pulled back and touched her forehead to his. "You gave me my life. Because of you, I am truly reborn. I can only hope one day to give you even a tiny bit of what you have given me. Our last year together has been beyond measure."

Rei's eyes opened wide. "Oh yeah. Hold that thought." He gently lifted Rome up and turned her around to sit her down. "Wait here," he said and he dashed out of the room. He came back a minute later with a big smile on his face and his hands behind his back.

"What?" Rome asked. "What do you have?" She craned her neck to peer around him.

"Just this."

He sank down one knee. "Rome," he said, holding his free hand out to her. Rome placed her hand in his without knowing why. "Will you marry me?" he asked.

As he was saying the words, he brought his other hand out to the front and showed her a deep burgundy velvet box. He popped the box open and contained inside was a ring made up of a platinum body complete with a large diamond on the top and two smaller trapezoidal diamonds along the side.

"I do not understand," she said, smiling, shaking her head. "We are already married. What is this?"

"This, my love, is an engagement ring. It's what a man of my generation would give to the woman who captured his heart. MINIMCOM got our molecular sequencers to make one for you."

Rome could not wipe the smile from her face. She lifted the ring out of the box and hefted it in her hand. She looked up at her husband and deadpanned, "What happens if I say no?"

"Oh," Rei said, crestfallen. "I hadn't thought of that."

"Well, the answer is yes, anyway," she said, her face beaming. "The same as the last time you asked me. But why?"

Rei laughed. "Why?" He showed her how to slide the ring over her finger. Rome held it up to the light and was fascinated by the way the ring sparkled. "The why is because I didn't do it right last time."

"I think we had extenuating circumstances."

"Yes, this is true. But there's one other thing."

"What?" Rome replied. "What more could there be?"

"I didn't pick today at random. Today is our one year anniversary, too," he said. "It was one year ago today that you and Canus thawed me out and we met for the first time. So this is an anniversary present, too."

"Oh Rei," Rome said, leaning forward, hugging him around the neck. "You are too much for me. I did not make anything for you."

"Oh yes you did." Rei pointed in the general direction of Aason's nursery.

"That does not count. Aason is for both of us."

"Rome," he explained, turning serious, "what you said before. You have already given me everything a man could ever want. It's enough."

"Not enough," said Rome. "I want to do something else. Name it. I will do anything."

Rei paused for a second. "Nothing comes to mind but I'll let you know when I think of it, OK?"

"Yes. Just tell me and I will do whatever you ask."

"You got it. In the meantime…"

"What?" Rome asked.

Rei smiled sheepishly. He reached down and pulled Rome up, moving his hands to her waist. Rei kissed her gently at first, then increasingly more passionately. Rome pressed in tightly, stroking his hair. His hands slid upward and caressed her in places that had been ignored for quite some time. Rei pulled back and looked into her eyes. Rome nodded demurely.

As Rei reached down to take her hand, Rome exclaimed, "Wait!"

"What?" he asked.

"Please remember that I just gave birth four days ago. While it is true that we Vuduri heal extremely quickly, you must be *very* gentle with me. It cannot be exactly what you are looking for."

"I love you," he said. "I just want to be with you. It doesn't matter how."

He swept Rome up into his arms. She smiled at him and put her arms around his neck, thinking back to their long hike when they first arrived at Deucado.

*"You always take care of me,"* she thought, purposefully using the cellphone that was in their heads.

*"Always,"* Rei thought back as he carried her into the bedroom. As they entered, he closed the door behind them. The action caused him to laugh at the absurdity of the action.

"Old habits die hard," he muttered.

"What?" Rome asked as he set her down by the bedside.

He jammed his thumb over his shoulder at the door. "Closing the door. Who is going to see us out here?"

"It is a good habit," Rome giggled as she began to unclasp the top part of her jumpsuit. "We are Aason's parents and what we do in here is not part of his business. This is just between you and me."

"Right," Rei said, stepping forward. He enveloped Rome in his arms and squeezed, holding on as if for dear life.

"What?" Rome asked as Rei was muzzling her neck.

"I love you so much," he said. "To this day, I still cannot believe I found you and that you are mine."

"Not to be too technical," she said, wriggling loose. "But I found you. I am the lucky one. As I said, you are the one that set me free."

"You didn't find me," Rei countered. "Your co-workers picked me out of my group. They brought me to you. I was the one selected."

"No," Rome said. "I was the one selected to communicate with you. You were selected at random."

"Random, my ass," he said. "I traveled 1400 years and 26 light years to find you. That kind of stuff just doesn't happen at random."

"What does your ass have to do with this?" Rome asked with a smile on her face. She put her arms around Rei and grabbed his butt with her hands and squeezed. "Although it is a very nice ass, I must add."

Rei laughed and hugged her back. He kissed her at the top of her cleavage and worked his way up until he reached the base of her neck. Rome tilted her head back to receive his kisses. Rei continued around until he reached the top of her shoulder. Rome was expecting him to move on but he seemed to get stuck there. She noticed Rei was sniffing her skin. She waited a moment longer and he became more and more intrigued until finally he actually licked her once.

"What are you doing?" Rome asked, completely puzzled.

"I love your smell, your taste," he replied. "I love everything about you."

"So what do I smell like? What do I taste like?"

"You smell wonderful. So clean, so sweet. Like vanilla surgical scrub."

"And what do I taste like?" Rome asked, amused by the whole thing.

"You taste like heaven, my love. Just like heaven."

Rome reached up and pulled Rei's head around so that she could kiss him. They were starting to get rather passionate when there was a knock at the door.

"WHAT THE HELL?" Rei shouted and jumped away from Rome.

"I am frightened," Rome whispered to Rei who was peering at the door with a wild look to his eye.

"Get in the bathroom," he whispered back. "And close the door."

"What will you do?"

"Go!" Rei commanded.

Rome tiptoed hurriedly toward the bathroom while Rei crept forward toward the entrance. He sidled around the dresser that was to the left of the door and picked up the onyx box that held the espansors, the bands that Rei and Rome used to connect mind to mind. It wasn't much of a weapon but it was all he could find.

"Who is it?" Rei asked, realizing the absurdity of the situation. At their current speed, they were probably one and a half light years away from Deucado by now, traveling faster than any manned ship in the history of mankind and buried inside the cargo compartment of an intelligent and deadly hybrid spaceship/computer dedicated to their safety.

"A-ma," came a muffled voice.

Rei pressed the stud and the door opened.

There was no one there. He looked up and down the hall but could see nothing.

"MINIMCOM," he said. "Are you playing a joke?"

"Nanhume boete," answered a ghostly voice from right in front of him. Rei jumped back.

Rome poked her head out of the refresher. "Beo?" she asked in Vuduri. "Is that you?"

The air shimmered in front of Rei and the disembodied head of Fridone appeared to float in front of him.

"Fridone?" Rei inquired, confused.

Fridone smiled and the rest of his body appeared. Immediately, Rei could see Rome's father was wearing one of the Deucadon's invisibility cloaks. Fridone was also holding Aason who was smiling.

"Aiee!," Rome shouted and rushed forward to hug her father. "What are you doing here?" she asked him.

"I told you. Somebody has to watch your son while you fight your fight."

"But Beo," Rome said sadly. "If they find you, they will know what is happening on Deucado. And we cannot take you back now."

"They will not find me, little Rome." Fridone pointed to the invisibility cloak. "They will not find me if they cannot see me," he said smiling.

"But Aason," Rome said. "What about him?"

"MINIMCOM and I had some discussions. He assured me that that we can do this with absolutely no danger to myself or Aason. I would not have come along if there was any chance of jeopardizing your mission."

There was a clicking sound from with the grille mounted to the left of the bed.

"Aason will be fine," MINIMCOM piped in. "Fridone and Aason can remain aboard me. I will eject your space tug well before their detection range. You will fly to Earth within your craft. With my new invisibility shell, no one will know we are here until we are ready to tell them."

Rei looked at Rome. Rome shrugged. He set the onyx box back on the dresser as he no longer needed the fearsome weapon.

"What about all the discomfort you mentioned before? About people traveling in your new cabin?" Rei directed to MINIMCOM.

"I will make the necessary adjustments. It will not be a problem," MINIMCOM replied, ending the subject.

"OK then," Rei said, shrugging. "It sounds like a plan to me."

"And to me as well," Rome replied, stroking Aason gently on his head.

"That makes three of us," Fridone said in Vuduri.

*"Me four,"* answered Aason as well, broadcasting to his mother using PPT modulation, to his father using their normal electromagnetic band and to Fridone, compliments of MINIMCOM

24

who relayed Aason's transmission and played it through his grille. Somehow, MINIMCOM made Aason's tiny voice sound like it suited his tiny body. It caused them all to laugh.

# Chapter 6

THE ONLY REAL ACCOMMODATION THAT ROME AND REI HAD TO make to account for their unanticipated passenger was a bit of rearranging of their small kitchen. They used the molecular sequencer to create an extra chair for Fridone so he could sit beside the combination carrier/high chair for Aason.

For the next six days, there wasn't much to do but spend time together as they traveled at an unimaginable speed toward Earth. On that sixth day, they found themselves approximately one light year away from their birth world, roughly one day out from the release point that MINIMCOM had determined was far enough away to avoid detection but near enough to minimize the time that Rei and Rome had to travel in the substantially slower space tug known as the Flying House.

Fridone and Rome were sitting at the dining table. Fridone was saying something when mid-sentence Rome held her hand up and Fridone stopped speaking. "I qua a, mau emir?" Rome asked Rei who was pacing furiously rocking Aason as he walked.

Rei turned to her. "It won't hold up," he answered in English.

"Vuduri, bir vefir," Rome replied, pointing to Fridone. "What will not hold up?" she asked in Vuduri.

"Our plan," he replied. "Our explanation as to what went down on Deucado. It is too complex. Lies are best kept simple."

"Which part is too complex?"

"The whole thing." Rei started ticking off his points with his fingers. "The way we have it, one, we flew to Deucado. Two, somehow we lost the Ark. Three, we met with some kind Vuduri people who escorted us ever so nicely to their compound. Four, somehow, they kept the whole conspiracy about the prison world a secret even while they reintegrated you into their samanda. Five, you gave birth and never discovered that anything was off there. Six, they just let us go when we decided to return to Earth for no particular reason." Rei waved his free hand in the air. "Rome," he said, "the pieces do not fit together. It is too complicated and that is a fundamental flaw."

"Cannot it be simply that they did not reintegrate me into their samanda?" she asked. "That way, I would not be able to detect their deception."

"Can you really pull that off? There is no way to detect that?"

"Their instruments will detect that my body is emanating PPT modulation but they would not be able to ascertain if it was due to reintegration or natural recovery."

"And you think it will hold up?"

"It held up against the Overmind of Deucado," Rome countered.

"But that was an Overmind made up of maybe one thousand Vuduri. You are going to go up against one built from half a billion minds."

"Nonetheless, I will be up to the task," Rome said firmly.

"OK, I am not going to argue with you about that. But what about Aason?"

"What about him?"

"Well, we were going to tell them that you gave birth on Deucado and now we are going to hide him on MINIMCOM? How do we explain that?"

"We will say that we left him behind," Rome answered back.

"With whom? With your father?" Rei asked. "We cannot say that because then we would know about the Ibbrassati and that gives the whole thing away again. So we would have to say we left Aason with somebody else. Rome, no offense intended, but nobody is going to believe that you left your baby behind with a perfect stranger. Why would we even leave Deucado in the first place?"

Rome looked at Fridone then back at Rei. "While I admit that there are some holes in our story, I think we can cover them up long enough to accomplish our goals."

"Maybe you can," he said. "But I am not such a good liar. I will mess up somehow. My parents taught me always to tell the truth."

"You lied convincingly to the Vuduri on Deucado regarding your Ark," Rome pointed out.

"No, I did not. They thought they were all so clever by reintegrating you and then probing your mind. Nobody ever bothered to ask me."

"Oh. Yes," Rome observed thoughtfully. "This is typical of the Vuduri. Given a problem, once they arrive at a solution, it would never occur to them to try a different approach."

"And look where it got them."

Rome nodded. "All right, then. If you do not think our story will work, do you have a better suggestion?"

"I think I do." Rei walked over to Fridone and handed him Aason. "I think I have a way of us not having to explain what happened on Deucado at all."

"How is that?" Rome asked.

"We just make it seem like we never even got there."

"But we did get there. I am not understanding you."

"You will," Rei said, sitting down. "Here…"

He swept all the dishes and silverware on the table off to the side. Then he started rearranging the plates and flatware that were sitting there one at a time.

"Let us say that this plate is Tabit," he said. He picked up a small plate and placed it at one end of the table.

"All right. Go on."

"OK. Our story starts there. The Stareater, the whole thing. We leave that part alone. So now we are traveling toward Deucado. Say that MINIMCOM and our Flying House towed the Ark a little past the star, Keid." With that, Rei put another plate to the right of the first one and laid a fork between the two plates. "That fork is our trajectory. MINIMCOM," he called out. "How long did that take?"

"Roughly seven months."

"All right. At that point, let us say you were already three months pregnant."

"I was," Rome replied with a smile on her face. "Remember, I was there."

"Sure, sure," Rei said. "So this is where we change what happened. Let us say that at that point, you and I decided we wanted the baby to be born on Earth. We would let MINIMCOM tow the Ark the rest of the way to Deucado by himself." He pushed another plate, slightly off from a straight line near the plate representing Keid. He took another fork and placed it to show the route taken by MINIMCOM and the Ark.

"So you and I never arrived at Deucado?" asked Rome.

"Exactly. That way there is no issue regarding our interaction with the Vuduri. There is nothing to explain because it never happened. We would not know about the Ibbrassati or anything that was going on there."

"What would prevent the Vuduri on Earth from going out and looking for the Ark?" Rome asked.

"Well, given this scenario," Rei said, "that would mean that right now, MINIMCOM and the Ark would be, like, six light years out from Deucado. MINIMCOM, how long would it take you to tow the Ark from that point to Deucado by yourself?

"Well over one year," MINIMCOM replied. "Assuming I could do it at all when I was just a tug."

"Well, we say you could. So no questions there. Nobody is going to go out and search for them, not in interstellar space like that. What would be the hurry? Besides, if they went to look, they'd get to Deucado first and know what was happening anyway."

"All right, Rei," Rome replied. "I understand so far. That takes care of Deucado. What about the rest. What were we doing while MINIMCOM was tasked with towing the Ark to Deucado?"

"That part is easy. We just say we made a beeline for Earth."

"What is a beeline?" asked Fridone.

"A straight line," Rei answered. He moved the final plate past the one representing Deucado so that, in totality, the arrangement represented a semi-circle. He lined up a knife from the plate representing Keid to the one representing Earth. "That would be our trajectory," he said, "in the Flying House."

"That seems simple enough," observed Fridone.

Rome studied his makeshift diagram. She shook her head. "There are two problems with that," she said.

"And what are the problems?" Rei asked.

"MINIMCOM, how long would it take us to travel from this supposed drop point back to Earth?" Rome asked.

"No more than three months assuming you were traveling at maximum speed."

"So Rei, this means we should have arrived at Earth months ago," Rome pointed out. "How would you explain our delay?"

"Easy," he replied. "We have MINIMCOM cripple our ship. Make it so that it can only push us along at a speed that corresponds to our arrival time."

"MINIMCOM, can you do this?"

"Yes. I could dampen down the strength of the Casimir pumps. They would be less effective. There would be less negative energy emitting from the PPT generators. Thus each tunnel would extend a shorter distance. This would have the net effect of reducing your overall effective speed."

"That is perfect, MINIMCOM, thanks," Rei replied. Then to Rome, he said, "What is the other problem?"

"Aason," she said, pointing at their son. "How would you explain his absence?"

Rei stood up and walked over to Rome. He squatted down and put both his hands on her shoulders, looking into her beautiful eyes. He caressed her gently for a moment, marveling at the peace he felt when he was in her presence. Then he took a deep breath.

"Romey, listen to me carefully," Rei said quietly. "Please do not get upset, but Aason died at childbirth."

"What!?" Rome shouted, "No! Not our baby," she said. Tears welled up in her eyes.

"Not for real," Rei said. "We are just saying that. He will be safe onboard MINIMCOM with your father. We just say he was stillborn."

"But even thinking this makes me so sad," Rome said. "It makes me cry. I would not..." She stopped speaking. Through her tears, a broad smile started to form. "I would be so sad that I would not be able to answer any questions without breaking down."

"Exactly," Rei said. "No muss, no fuss. All bases covered."

"I am so sorry, baby," Aason's mother said wiping away her tears. She turned toward her son. "It hurts me to even think about this," she said.

*"It will be all right, Mother,"* Aason replied. *"I understand."*

"All right. Beo?" Rome asked. "What do you think?"

"I think that Rei's parents did not do such a good job to teach him to always tell the truth. These lies come very easy," he said with a smile.

"But it will work?" Rei asked.

"It will work," replied Fridone.

"MINIMCOM?" Rei asked. "What do you think? Any obvious flaws?"

`"Just one."`

"And what is that?" asked Rome.

`"Your nursery. If anyone should come aboard and examine your ship, they will know what it was for and they will see that it was used."`

"Well, just having it should not be a problem. Would we not get it ready in advance of the baby being born?" Rei asked.

`"I think it would be more effective to just remove it,"` replied MINIMCOM. `"You will not need it any more as I will prepare facilities for Aason onboard me. It would be simpler to leave no evidence. Just say you took it down because of the sadness it caused by leaving it in place."`

"All right," Rei agreed. "We will take down the nursery. Anything else? Do you think the story is tight?"

`"Yes,"` replied the computer/spaceship. `"Your suggested modifications make it the simplest story and therefore will take the longest to penetrate with inconsistencies. I will deploy a modest number of starprobes in this general region. I will be able to detect any ships that are launched to investigate. I should be able to give you some advance warning should there be any suspicion of untruth."`

"That is a good idea," Rome said. "Let us get started."

All three got up and went about preparing the ship to stand up to even a detailed inspection. Fridone and Rei set to work dismantling the nursery. Rome exited the Flying House, into MINIMCOM's cargo compartment which had been pressurized for Fridone. Carrying Aason's high chair, Rome made her way to the "new" super-sized MINIMCOM to examine the facilities that he had erected for Aason and her father. After she was satisfied, she came back on board the Flying House and reviewed the sensor logs and other data storage formats to make sure there was no evidence that Fridone or Aason were ever aboard their converted tug.

# Chapter 7

TWELVE HOURS LATER, REI AND ROME WERE DRESSED IN THEIR pressure suits, strapped into the high-G harnesses in the cockpit of the Flying House. Their instrumentation told them that MINIMCOM had begun pumping the air out of the cargo hold and their ship would soon be sitting in the vacuum of space.

"Stand by for release," MINIMCOM instructed.

"Wait," Rome said, suddenly panicking. "I am not ready yet. MINIMCOM, I need to see Aason and my father again."

"*Mother, I will be all right. I am with Grandbeo*," said Aason in her mind.

"*That is not the point, baby*," Rome thought back. "I need to see you one last time," she said out loud.

One of the viewscreens flickered and she could see Aason and her father sitting in MINIMCOM's cockpit which was much roomier than before.

"Beo, Aason," Rome said in Vuduri. "We will call you when we have arranged our affairs and it is time to approach Earth. We will land and make contact with Mea. She will broadcast the situation on Deucado to the Vuduri population in general. Once that occurs, it will be safe for you to join us."

She turned her attention to the grille built into the control panel. "MINIMCOM, you have the exact formula, correct?" she said, cupping her left breast.

"Yes, Rome," MINIMCOM said with infinite patience. "You do realize this is the twelfth time that you have asked me that."

Rei grinned wryly. "That's Mom talking, not Rome, MINIMCOM. Moms are born to worry," he said.

"Clearly."

Rei reached over and touched Rome's gloved hand with his own. "Are you ready, Mommy?" he asked.

"No. But yes. I am as ready as I will ever be."

"All right, MINIMCOM, start the separation sequence," Rei called out.

"Roger."

Rei chuckled to himself and wondered where that one came from. In the viewscreens that projected an image from the aft cameras, they could see a horizontal crack appear across the back end of the cargo bay. The crack widened and widened until they could see the full expanse of space behind them.

"Neutralizing artificial gravity."

"Roger," Rei said back to MINIMCOM returning the gibe.

There was the slightest of shuddering as their craft lifted off the flat surface of the cargo deck. Looking forward out of the windshield, the only thing Rei and Rome could see was the gray wall of the cargo compartment bulkhead.

"I will move forward. Your ship will remain exactly where it is. Do not fire your engines until there is sufficient distance between us."

"Of course," Rei replied.

The forward bulkhead began to move away from them and through the viewscreens projecting behind them, they came closer and closer to the star field until the edges of MINIMCOM's cargo door and ramp were no longer visible. They turned their attention to the front windows and saw the most peculiar sight. Buried within the star field was the dimly lit interior of MINIMCOM's cargo bay, yet there was nothing around it. The lighted edges grew smaller and smaller.

"You are free," MINIMCOM said. "Let me move off."

The cargo ramp and door closed. Within seconds, there was nothing but empty space.

"That is so weird, MINIMCOM," Rei said. "If I didn't know any better, I'd swear you were never there."

"That is the point," replied the computer/spaceship. "I am now 50 meters above you in the Z axis and climbing. I will keep my shell visible to MIDAR until you are past."

"All right," Rei said. He looked over at Rome. Without even reading her mind, he could see the complex interplay of emotions flying over her face. "It'll be OK, sweetheart," he said in English.

"I know," Rome replied. "But it is hard."

"Well, the sooner we go, the sooner we can all be together, right?"

"Right," she said.

Rei turned back to the controls. A quick check of the MIDAR screen showed that MINIMCOM was moving away from them vertically at a steady clip. Rei used his tug's trim-jets to move them forward and away until they were several thousand meters apart. He reached forward and pressed the icon for the preset sequence of the old-fashioned turn-stop-turn-jump. Soon they heard the high-pitched whine of the PPT generators coming up to speed. A thin black circle appeared in front of them. Only the edge eclipsed the stars. From this angle, it was hard to tell that it was a PPT tunnel at all since the stellar density was the same inside and out. Rei punched the throttle to ignite the plasma jets and they were pushed back in their seats. As soon as they emerged from the tunnel, Rei cut the plasma thrusters, allowing them to coast. He turned toward Rome. "How'd we do?" he asked.

"My bloco and stilo are no longer functional, as you will recall," Rome said, tapping her temple. "I will check but I must do it manually."

"Sure."

"Please wait while I overlay the theoretical on top of the actual trajectory," she stated. She typed several commands into the viewscreen and connected several points of arc. A smile crept across her face.

"Perfect!" she said. "50c right on the mark. Very good, mau emir." She looked at Rei's face. "For an amateur, that is."

"Amateur!" Rei said in mock surprise. "I've been flying this stupid ship for over a year. I should be getting good at it by now."

"Technically, it was MINIMCOM who was flying it most of the time," Rome countered. "And you will recall when we had to make the emergency landing on Deucado, you made me fly the tug down."

"Whatever," Rei replied dismissively. "This part I'm good at so let me have my glory."

He committed the sequence within the autopilots memory and gave it the command to repeat until they were well inside the orbit of Mars. The actual distance remaining to the Earth would be about 35 million kilometers. After that, they would fly manually.

"How long do we have?" Rei asked Rome. "On autopilot, I mean."

"Approximately eight hours," she replied after studying the instrumentation. "That will get us close enough to where the ship will require our attention again."

"So," Rei said, looking at her intently, "what are we going to do with eight hours to kill?"

Rome smiled. She unclasped the high-G harness and stood up. "I am Vuduri," she said proudly, straightening up and thrusting her shoulders back. "We heal very quickly. I believe you and I have some unfinished business to attend to. May I assume that you are still interested?" she asked in her most seductive voice.

"Am I ever?" Rei said, practically tearing the harness off him and jumping up.

Rome held out her hand. They found plenty of what to do as the autopilot moved them inexorably toward Earth, one jump at a time.

Eight hours later, they were back in the cockpit, smiles on their faces. To keep questions to a minimum, Rome had elected to put on a traditional white Vuduri jumpsuit. Rei was wearing a brown short-sleeved shirt and tan slacks.

They watched the jump counter intently as it neared zero. Each time the ship punched through a tunnel, Rei craned his neck trying to see the Earth.

"Where is it?" he said finally, somewhat impatiently.

"Where is what?" Rome deadpanned.

"Earth. Come on, honey, you knew that."

"Yes," she said laughing. She pointed at the front windshield. "There," she said, "that bright blue dot. That is no star. That is the Earth."

Her fingers flew over the touch screen. Cascading circles collapsed onto a single blue pixel in the middle of the screen. "One more jump should do it," she said. "Then it will be plasma thrusters the rest of the way."

"Oh boy," Rei said excitedly. "I haven't been here in 1400 years. I wonder if the place has changed much."

Rome scrunched up her expression and shook her head gently. The ship rotated about its center axis and fired its plasma thrusters, bringing them to a complete halt. She disengaged the autopilot.

"All right, Rei, last time," she said.

"Gotcha," Rei replied. He rotated the craft so that the front faced toward the Earth. A quick press of a button fired up the PPT projectors. Rei punched the plasma thrusters and they were through. There, in front them, like a tiny blue jewel with just a hint of frosting, lay the Earth.

"Woo hoo!" Rei said, giddy for reasons he really didn't understand. "There's the Moon, too!" he said, pointing. "You don't know how weird this is, honey."

"Why?" she asked.

"Because when I left, I thought I was never coming back. It just wasn't in the cards."

"Many parts of our lives are strange and inexplicable," Rome said. "You seem to have developed the ability to take things, in stride, I believe you would say."

"Yeah," Rei said thoughtfully. The smile slowly left his face, only to be replaced by a more somber look.

"What?" she asked. "I thought this would make you happy. You get to see the Earth again."

"Your Earth, not mine. All my family…"

"Do not become morose," Rome said kindly. "I do not mean to be insensitive but we have a job to do. Let us do it."

Rei sighed. "You're right." He squeezed the button for the plasma thrusters down hard and they were pushed back in their seats as the spaceship accelerated toward their home planet.

"Easy," Rome said. "We will be entering the traveling lanes shortly."

Rei took his thumb off the plasma thruster control and the engines cut out. "How long before they pick us up?" he asked. "On MIDAR or whatever?"

"I have already detected some sounding beacons. Look, there," she said, pointing at some flashing yellow patterns moving across the main viewscreen. "That is a handshake request. They know we are here."

"What do we do?" Rei asked.

"I think we should let them bring us in. It would be safest that way."

Rei looked at Rome. "Safe is good. We have no reason to not let them, right?"

"No," Rome said. "We would only raise suspicion if we resist."

"So, let 'er rip."

Rome nodded and pressed several buttons then pulled her hands off the controls. The plasma thrusters came on of their own accord and they began to accelerate toward Earth, a bit more gently than before. By careful observation, it was clear to Rei from the intricate dance of the engines and trim-jets that a skilled pilot, albeit several hundreds of thousands of kilometers away, was bringing them home.

"Is that a computer or a person doing that," Rei asked, pointing at the display screen.

"It would be one of OMCOM's brothers," Rome said. "It would make no sense to have a human try and pilot the ship. If that were the case, they would just let us operate the controls."

"I see what you mean," he agreed.

Time passed very quickly and it wasn't long until the blue jewel was the brightest object in the sky. Their progress was palpable and mesmerizing. Rei punched up a magnified view of their target and stared at the globe in front of him with its puffy white clouds and surface made mostly of water. The continents looked identical to when Rei left.

It took them less than an hour. The unseen pilot cut back on the thrusters and the trim-jets executed a roll and yaw maneuver that altered their course so that they entered orbit going east to west, the opposite of what Rei expected. Below them was the vast blue of the Pacific. Billowy white clouds hung off the shore but the central Pacific was perfectly clear.

"Look, there," Rome said, pointing at the front console. "We have company."

Rei could see two blips heading right toward the center of the MIDAR screen. "Do we need the side cameras?" Rei asked.

"Not necessary," she answered as she craned her head around to see past the side window. Rei did the same. The ships that were now alongside them were something more than tugs and something less than interstellar ships.

"What are they?" he asked, turning back to the viewscreen to study their sensor data.

"They are transports," Rome replied. "Similar to the Algol but smaller, faster."

"Why do you think they are here?"

"I do not know," she answered. "Perhaps this is just caution on their part."

"Well, Ursay and the gang have been back for a long time. They know who we are, right?"

"Absolutely," Rome said, never taking her eyes off the ship to her right. "I do not see any sign of weapons so I do not think they are hostile."

"Well, the Vuduri really don't have any enemies around here anyway and we certainly don't look like Stareaters. I think maybe we're just nervous because we don't have innocent eyes."

Rome turned to look at him. "What do you mean innocent eyes?"

"Well, we know what has happened so we can never see things the same again. We project that on others even though they would have no cause for suspicion."

"I understand," Rome said. "Maybe they are just making sure we arrive safely. After all, they know how far we have come."

"Yeah, that must be it," Rei said, only half-convinced.

After achieving low Earth orbit, the autopilot, under control of unseen forces on the ground, executed a series of swoops and dives, which allowed them to shed their excess velocity without having to resort to a brute force assault on the atmosphere and eliminating the need for any kind of heat-resistant surfaces. Most of their velocity was shed over Asia. When they were traveling perhaps at Mach 2, they began their descent in earnest, toward Eastern Europe. As they got deeper in the atmosphere, the EG lifters took over and the aerodynamic surfaces asserted their control.

Peering out the window, Rei asked, "Is there anything left of our cities, you know, from my time?"

"No," replied Rome. "I am not sure of the proper word. They were...erased."

"Oh." he said. He sat there quietly for a moment staring down at the Mediterranean Sea. The boot of Italy looked the same as it always did. "Where do you think they are taking us?" he asked.

"I-cimaci, I would presume," Rome replied, pointing ahead to the horizon. As they got lower, Rei recognized the distinctive shape of the Iberian Peninsula and Spain, bordered by the Mediterranean on one side and the Atlantic Ocean on the other. Passing even lower, they flew over the straits of Gibraltar then up along the coast, past where Cadiz and Seville had been located in Rei's time. The Atlantic Ocean stretched off to the left as far as the eye could see. Where the coastline jutted out into the ocean, they cut inland heading due north. At one point, without remembering his geography perfectly, Rei guessed they were now over what had been Portugal.

Lower and lower they flew. Ahead of them, Rei could make out ring-like structures, interrupted by crossing lines. He remembered seeing pictures of I-cimaci during their year-long voyage to Deucado. The city was built like a bull's-eye with eight major roads crisscrossing the center. As they got closer, he could see block-like buildings lying in the spaces between the roads. Off in the distance, he could see a single, giant shining structure.

"That is The Tower," Rome said. "It is the tallest one on Earth."

Rei recognized it immediately. The immense spire was the only structure of all the Vuduri architecture that was of any note. He had seen many pictures of this future Earth but it was nothing like seeing it in person. The Vuduri had absolutely no imagination when it came to urban planning or habitat design. The starbase on Dara was built along the exact same plan as their major cities, circular hallways, crossing corridors and the like.

"That is the Rio Tejo," Rome said, pointing the bay to the right of the city. "The spaceport is near the water just past the edge of the city. There."

Below them were hundreds of air and spacecraft lined up in neat rows alongside some low-lying buildings. They looped around to a wide, flat area on the far side of one building. Finally, their forward velocity came to a halt about 50 feet above the ground. The indicators on the front panel showed their landing gear was being extended. Their tug began descending straight down.

Rei looked to the left and right and saw their escorts had followed them all the way down. They experienced a slight jolt and the main display indicated they had landed.

"Time to get this show on the road!" Rei said, unbuckling his harness.

"Yes, the show," Rome said a bit more glumly. "Remember," she said. "Trust no one and say nothing until we find my mother."

"Yes, dear," Rei said with a sigh. He moved over to Rome and bent down. "Do you need help getting up?" he asked her.

"No," she said. "Why do you ask that?"

"I recall that last time you were a little more stuck in your seat."

"Oh yes. I recall this as well." She reached up for him and pulled him down to her. She kissed him and said, "Rei, no matter what happens, know that I love you."

"I know you do, honey. I love you too," he replied, puzzled. "We'll be OK. Let's get you up."

She nodded and released her high-g harness and stood.

"How do you feel," he said.

"I think I am afraid," she replied. "We have a tall task in front of us."

"Eh, that?" Rei said. "We just have a planet to conquer. No big deal."

"Yes, no big deal," Rome said wryly.

Together, hands against the walls, they made their way down the hallway.

"There's a whole boatload of déjà vu going on here, isn't there?" Rei asked.

"Déjà vu?" she questioned as they made their way to the far end of the cargo compartment.

"Yeah, been there, done that."

"I suppose. But our landing was a bit more controlled this time as opposed to last time. Our descent to Deucado was rather rough. And thankfully, no ice."

"Yep," Rei answered. He pushed the blue stud to raise the cargo door and lower the ramp. Compared to the dim light of the ship during their travel, the sunlight flooding their cargo compartment from their home star was very bright. So much so that Rei had to hold his arm up to shield his eyes. Of course, with Rome's advanced optics, she had no such problem.

Rei just shut his eyes, figuring it was easier to let his eyes adjust that way. Rome reached up and tugged his arm.

"Rei," she said.

"Yeah, I'll be OK. I just need a minute to let my eyes adjust."

"REI!" Rome said, insistently.

"What?"

Even though his eyes were blurry from the brightness, Rei blinked a few times until his vision cleared.

There standing at the base of the ramp was an angry-looking phalanx of soldiers holding sleek rifles, pistols plus a variety of other harsh-looking weapons that Rei did not recognize. All of them pointed at the space-faring couple.

"Does this remind you of anything?" he asked Rome, slowly raising his hands above his head.

"Unfortunately, yes," she replied, doing the same.

When they got to the base of the ramp, one of the soldiers walked up to them and spoke haltingly in Vuduri, "Rome, you are under arrest."

Rome nodded once and lowered her arms. Two armed guards moved around past the first soldier's side and took Rome by the arms. Firmly, they pulled at Rome and began marching her away from the bottom of the tug's ramp toward a transport parked about 30 feet away.

"Why are you arresting her?" Rei asked. "What did she do?"

The soldier looked at Rei. He cleared his throat several times but clearly speaking was not one of his strong points. "She facilitated an OMCOM to become Tasanceti."

"Tasanceti?" Rei asked and then his heart sank. "Oh. Yeah."

"You must come with us as well," the soldier said in a gravelly voice.

"Am I under arrest, too?"

"No, you are a hero. We just need to ask you some questions."

"Some hero," Rei muttered under his breath, starting forward alongside the soldier.

# Chapter 8

THE TRANSPORT WAS LITTLE MORE THAN A FLYING CART WITH three rows of seats. Two soldiers sat in the front. Rei sat next to Rome in the middle row and a soldier sat on either side of them. The rear row was empty. They left the airfield and headed northeast, toward I-cimaci and the giant, looming tower that the Vuduri, in their infinite creativity, called The Tower. Rei craned his neck to gawk at the city ahead. As they passed the outskirts of the city, they passed row after row of one-story, long block-like structures.

"What are those?" Rei asked, pointing at the buildings.

Rome looked to where he was pointing. "Residences," she said.

"They look like prisons," Rei observed. "Just a door and one tiny window."

"That is how the Vuduri live," she replied.

Rei shrugged. They entered the city proper. It seemed rather deserted for what Rei knew to be its size. As they passed street after street, the occasional Vuduri stopped to look at them, but mostly they were ignored. Along the streets, there were some vehicles parked here and there. It was deadly quiet. The only noise was the sound of the wind as they moved through the streets.

As they traveled deeper into the city, Rei swiveled his head back and forth.

"Um, Rome?" he asked.

"What?"

"Where are all your robots?" Rei asked.

"What do you mean?"

"Robots. Automatons. Mechanical men."

"I understand what the word means," she said. "Why would you expect there to be robots?"

"Well, you guys are from the future and this is the city of tomorrow," he said. "Surely you have robots everywhere doing things, right? Obviously, you have the technology."

"Of course we have the technology," she replied. "But no robots. You will remember from your history lessons that the last time we had them, it did not end well. So now we do not have them. They are banned forever."

"Couldn't you make them safer or something?"

Rome took a deep breath. "They were one of the primary weapons used by MASAL during the war. They caused much death."

"Oh, yeah," he said. "MASAL."

"Yes, MASAL," Rome said in a hurt tone.

"What about the three laws of robotics?" Rei asked. "Couldn't you build those in?"

Rome shook her head. "I do not know anything about robot laws. All I know is that we entrusted the operation of the robots to MASAL and he turned them against us."

"So…" Rei started.

"So - never again," Rome said sharply. "The Vuduri will never have robots again. We could never trust them. Not in the cities. Not on the farms. Not at sea. Not anywhere."

"Even here?"

"Especially here," she said. "I-cimaci is what you might call the capital of the Earth."

"Huh," Rei observed then he quieted down. He twisted in place and craned his neck to stare up at the top of The Tower as it receded into the distance. Rei estimated that it was about a half-kilometer tall. While the building was not as tall as some of the skyscrapers of his day, it was impressive nonetheless.

After a time, they left the city proper and entered a fairly large wooded area. In front of them lay an unpaved path cut through the woods. The path looked fairly fresh, almost new. The trees along the road showed light core where the bark had been removed and had not yet regrown. The flying cart continued on until they came to a sizeable clearing. They pulled up to single-story U-shaped building that, not surprisingly, had no windows. The outside was made of stone rather than the ubiquitous aerogel that seemed to be the Vuduri norm. The architecture was as plain as could be. It had a fortress feel about it. The cart settled to the ground and the guards ushered Rome and Rei into the building. As they approached, the air smelled like fresh stone or concrete. Everything about this venue seemed new.

As they entered the building, two of the four soldiers remained behind and the other two soldiers walked them down corridor after corridor until they came to a doorway. One soldier opened the door and indicated to Rome that she should enter the vestibule. Rei started to go with her but the second soldier lowered his weapon and held it across Rei's middle.

The soldier cleared his throat and spoke with a surprisingly clear voice. "You will be able to join her in a short time. We need to ask you some questions first. Please follow me," he said. Rei looked at his eyes. One seemed dark but they were not as mismatched as Estar's or Sussen's. Further, the soldier seemed affable, for a Vuduri. He led Rei into the next room. The room itself was completely empty with the exception of a desk and two chairs, one on each side of the desk. The soldier pointed to the nearer chair.

"Oronus will be joining you shortly."

"Who is Oronus?" Rei asked.

"He is our arbiter. A Juoz," the soldier said. "Now please sit."

"A Juoz is a judge, right?" Rei asked in English. The soldier did not answer so Rei did as he was told. The soldier took a position to the left of the door. The windowless walls were all white, as was the floor. The ceiling had no visible light source but rather the entire ceiling glowed with a soft white light, giving the room an even illumination. In one corner, there was a white quarter-sphere attached where the ceiling met two walls. It reminded Rei of something but he couldn't quite put his finger on it.

Soon an older Vuduri man entered the room. He was carrying a thin notepad. He walked around to the far side of the desk and sat down, placing his pad on the table. He spent an uncomfortably long time studying the tablet, which was obviously electronic in nature. Finally, he spoke up.

"Asdiu Oronus," the man said then corrected himself, "I am Oronus."

"Fica bita veler am Vuduri," Rei said. "I understand it."

"Impressive," replied the man, "but no matter. English is perfectly suitable."

"What do you want?" Rei asked, surprised yet again how quickly English had spread throughout the Vuduri universe.

45

"As you are well aware, I am but a vessel for the Overmind," answered Oronus. "I was selected because my vocal apparatus is best suited to speaking and we have decided to ask you a few questions."

"What about Rome," Rei interjected. "When can I see her?"

"Shortly," replied the man. "Just answer our questions and we will take you to her."

*"Rome?"* Rei called to his wife, using the cellphone in his head. *"Are you there?"* There was no answer.

"What did you do to her?" Rei asked worriedly.

"We have done nothing to her. She is safe," Oronus answered. "She is not in any immediate danger."

"What does that mean?" Rei asked.

"For now, just know she is isolated in the room next door. When our business is concluded here, we will allow you to rejoin her."

"Why are you keeping her in isolation?" Rei asked.

"Her behavior has made her a danger for contact with all Vuduri," said Oronus, spreading his hands. "We do not wish to expose any more of our people to her than absolutely necessary."

"Rome is not a danger," Rei said. "The whole crime thing. She just did what she had to do. You already know that."

"Enough about Rome, please," the man answered sharply. "We will get to her soon enough. Please allow us to ask our questions."

"All right," Rei said, sighing. "Go ahead."

"Thank you," replied Oronus. "How did it happen that you are here on Earth? The last report we had was that you were going to tow the Essessoni Ark to Deucado. By our calculations, you should still be en route right now."

Rei's expression turned grim. "We had to let the Ark go. MINIMCOM is still towing it to Deucado, as far as I know."

"Why did you have to let the Ark go?" Oronus asked, confused.

"Uh…" Rei hesitated. "Rome became pregnant and there were some difficulties. We decided it would be better for her to give birth on Earth."

A hint of surprise flashed across Oronus's face. He looked down at the tablet and a series of dots and notations formed. He turned the tablet around and pushed it toward Rei. He unfastened a stylus from the side of the tablet and handed it to Rei.

"Show me your release point," he said, "where you and the MINIMCOM parted ways."

Rei studied the tablet. He saw dots representing Tabit, Keid, Deucado and Earth. There was a faint green line connecting Tabit to Deucado. Rei took the stylus and pressed it on the screen, leaving a blue mark, just to the right of Keid.

"Here," Rei said. "We released the Ark right about there."

Oronus looked down where Rei was pointing. A faint blue line connected the dot to Earth. Some numbers appeared on the screen. A yellow number with a negative sign in front of it started flashing.

"That is not correct," Oronus said.

"What's not..." Rei started to speak but Oronus held his hand up.

"Do not speak," Oronus interrupted him. His eyes defocused. A minute went by then another and other. Fully 10 minutes elapsed before Oronus finally blinked and then looked at Rei again.

"We have just examined your ship. What happened to your PPT generators?" he asked. "They are impaired."

"I don't know" Rei answered. "It's your ship. Maybe it wasn't designed to go such a long distance. It just sort of ran out of gas. There really wasn't anybody to ask."

Oronus sighed. The tablet cleared. He leaned forward slightly. "Rome is clearly not pregnant. Where is your baby?" Oronus asked.

Rei stuck his lip out. His shoulders slumped down. Very quietly, he said, "He...he was stillborn. There is no baby." Rei bit his lip so hard that a tear came to his eyes. He dabbed at it slowly to make sure that Oronus saw.

"Why would you even think to have a child in the first place?"

"It was not planned," Rei replied. "It just sort of happened."

"I see. When did the baby die?"

"A couple of weeks ago," Rei answered. "We almost made it except for the damned tug. We couldn't get here in time."

"Where is the body of the child?" Oronus asked. "Did you preserve it?"

Rei swallowed hard. This was one item they hadn't discussed. He thought about the Vuduri and their strange practices and took a guess.

"We put it in the recycler. Rome told me that was the only way to honor the dead. It seemed a little cold to me but that is your way, right?"

"Yes," Oronus said without any emotion. Rei let his shoulders relax.

"Tell me about your encounter with the Stareater," Oronus asked. "There is a recording on your ship that would indicate that the VIRUS units were successful in destroying it."

"Yes," Rei said, brightening. "OMCOM contacted us and told us that it was dead."

"OMCOM," Oronus harrumphed with disgust. "What else did he tell you?"

"He said there was a problem with the VIRUS units mutating. He said he was going to try and get the situation under control."

"Did he give you any more detail?" Oronus asked stridently. "After Ursay returned, we knew exactly what he was planning. Your recordings confirmed it. Puh."

"The only other thing he said was something about sentient beings, going off on their own," Rei muttered. "I don't remember exactly. It didn't really make sense to me but you said you had the recordings, right?"

"Yes," Oronus said. "But your impressions are valuable nonetheless."

"Well, it was like a year ago so I'm a little fuzzy on it. It wasn't a very long conversation as I recall."

"I understand," Oronus replied, pressing a point on the tablet with the stylus. "Do your best to dictate the conversation as faithfully as you can remember."

"I just did," Rei said. "It was only two or three sentences. He said he was happy to see us. He said the VIRUS units killed the Stareater. He said there were some mutations but he was working on it. Then he hung up."

"Nothing else?" Oronus asked skeptically.

"Not that I remember." Rei looked off to the side then up to the ceiling. He scanned the entire ceiling then brought his eyes back to regard Oronus. "Nope. That's it."

"Very well," Oronus said. "Have you had any contact with OMCOM since then?"

"Uh, no," Rei stuttered. "Nothing since."

Oronus nodded. Again his eyes defocused. Oronus' head sagged downward then snapped up again. "What were MINIMCOM's instructions regarding disposition of your Ark when it arrives at Deucado?" he asked finally.

"He was supposed to contact the Vuduri there and get their help in carting my people down to the surface," Rei said. "The Ark was pretty messed up and there is no way it could fly down on its own."

Oronus's expression tightened.

"They'll do that, right?" Rei asked sounding earnest.

"Yes, of course," Oronus said with no hesitation. "It will be taken care of." With that, the door opened and a soldier entered.

"We are finished here," Oronus said, standing. "Please remain with Grus until we call for you." He gathered up his tablet and walked out of the room, followed by the armed guard.

Rei stood and Grus led him out to an alcove next to the room where Rome was being held. Rei saw Oronus and the guard enter the vestibule and the door closed behind them. Grus pointed to the bench.

"Sanda-sa," Grus said. "Sit."

Rei sat down. "*Rome?*" he called again from inside his head. Again, there was no answer.

"Is Rome still in there?" Rei asked, pointing to the door.

"Som," replied Grus. "Eguerta. Wait."

Rei leaned back against the wall. He closed his eyes and tried another tack. He used his sonar-vision but it gave him no more information about Rome's condition, nor would it if the room they were holding her in was sound-proofed. He opened his eyes. Then it came to him.

"*Aason,*" he called out using his telephone circuit. "*Are you there? Are you close enough to hear me?*"

*"Yes, Father,"* his son replied faintly. *"We are in orbit around the Earth. Where is Mother?"*

*"You can't reach her either?"* Rei asked. *"Your connection?"*

*"No. The connection stopped,"* replied the baby. *"She told me they were taking her into a room then I heard nothing. I cannot hear any voices, not hers, not anyone's."*

*"Are you OK otherwise?"*

*"Yes, Father. Grandbeo and I are fine. Father, what is happening?"*

*"I am right outside the room where your mother is being held. They are going to let me see her shortly."*

*"That is good. Please tell I her I love her and that I miss her."*

*"I will,"* replied Rei, breaking off the connection. *"MINIMCOM, you there?"* he asked mentally.

"`Yes,`" replied the spaceship/computer.

*"Can you reach Rome? Why can't I contact her?"*

"`No, I cannot contact her,`" answered MINIMCOM. "`I have created an artificial triangulation receiver but I cannot detect any carrier wave in the vicinity other than yours.`"

*"I am literally sitting right outside the room where they are holding Rome. What's up with that?"*

"`It would appear the room you are referring to is a Faraday cage. I presume from Aason's comments that it is under T-suppression as well.`"

*"Faraday cage? T-suppressors!"* Rei's expression grew grim. *"They are serious about cutting her off."*

"`Will you be able to get in to see her?`" asked MINIMCOM.

*"They said I would,"* Rei replied. *"Hold on..."* he said as he noticed a commotion down the hallway.

Rei leaned forward to see three people walking briskly toward him, a woman and two men. Each of the men had a hand on the shoulders of the woman but she marched ahead, oblivious to their attempts at restraint. When they got to Rei, they stopped. The woman looked down at him and smiled. The two men released her shoulders and stepped back.

Rei looked up at her. She seemed very familiar. He racked his brain trying to remember if she was one of the crew members on Tabit but no, there was something else. The woman was little over five feet tall, standard height for a Vuduri. She had beautiful shoulder length brown hair with strands of gold and gray. She was wearing a regular issue Vuduri white jumpsuit that fit her form perfectly. Rei would have guessed she was in her forties but she looked extremely well preserved. Even though he was hopelessly and completely in love with Rome, Rei found the woman attractive in a way he could not explain. Rei looked into her dark, glowing eyes and found there was something about her bearing that was almost regal. It gave her an aura of power that Rei could not deny.

Not knowing what else to do, Rei stood up. The woman held out her arms. She reached out and pulled Rei in to hug him, kissing him gently on the cheek. "I am Binoda," she said.

Rei's jaw dropped, and then a great big smile broke out. "Asdiu dei valoz am cinhaca-li," he said.

"You may speak English to me," she replied. She turned to the other men standing by her.

"Filder ei lergi. Quari brofecoteta," she said in a commanding voice, although it had to be for Rei's benefit. The men backed up a little.

Rei asked quietly. "What's the point of talking in private?"

She leaned over and whispered in his ear, "I disconnected from the Overmind the moment your ship landed and I learned where they were taking you and my daughter. I am not connected right now." She turned and glared at the three men. They took another step backwards.

"Sit," Binoda said to Rei.

Rei sat down and Binoda sat next to him.

"Rome is in that room?" she asked, pointing to the door.

"Yes," he answered. "What are you doing here?"

Binoda just stared at him.

"I guess that is a stupid question, huh?" Rei offered.

"Wait," Binoda said. "Quenti a qua bissi fa-le?" she said, turning to Grus.

"Conci monudis," Grus replied gruffly.

"Very well," Binoda replied turning back to Rei. "We will be quiet for now."

"But, but," he said, ineffectively.

"Shh," Binoda said to him, putting two fingers up to her lips. "For now, we wait."

# Chapter 9

INSIDE THE COURTROOM, ROME SAT QUIETLY WHILE ORONUS looked at the tablet in front of him. An armed guard stood by the door. After studying the tablet for a while, Oronus spoke.

"I am Oronus. Before we get to your crimes, I need to ask you a few questions."

"Of course," Rome replied. She folded her hands in front of her and set them on the table. Her ring sparkled even in the subdued lighting of the all-white chamber. Oronus noticed it immediately.

"Why are you wearing that, that ring on your finger?" he asked.

"It is called an engagement ring," Rome replied. "Rei gave it to me as a promise."

"A promise for what?"

"Cesa," Rome replied. "He and I desire to be married."

"Vuduri do not marry," Oronus said curtly.

"But mandasurte do," answered Rome. "I was Cesdiud. I am no longer one of you."

"You appear to be rather proud of that fact," Oronus observed. "I would think you would be ashamed."

"I am not," Rome replied defiantly. "It has liberated me."

"This room is under continuous T-suppression," said Oronus. "I am disconnected right now. I do not know about you but I find it extraordinarily uncomfortable."

"I do agree, when it first happened to me, I found it very disconcerting," she said. "But after a short while, I got used to it and now I would not give it up for the world."

"Why?" Oronus asked, confused. "Why would anybody want to live this way?"

"Because it allows me to have my own thoughts and my own feelings. I do not have to share them with anyone."

"What about the Overmind?" he asked.

"Especially the Overmind," Rome fired back. "It is the unrelenting inspection of one's thoughts and feelings by the Overmind that turn the Vuduri into unthinking automatons. We are too proud of a people to ever risk having an idea or an emotion that might be embarrassing so we suppress them all. This is not a good thing."

"I disagree. It is a very good thing," countered Oronus. "Without it, all of society would get unruly, uncontrolled. Look at the mandasurte. Emotions only get in the way of efficiency."

"You cannot know this," Rome said sympathetically, "but by giving up feelings, we have relinquished a part of our humanity, a part of our soul, really. We are diminished as a species."

"I believe we are elevated," said Oronus in an acerbic voice.

"I think you are wrong," replied Rome.

"I am not wrong," insisted Oronus. "What evidence do you have?"

"I will tell you but you will not believe me," Rome said.

"Please," scoffed Oronus. "Try to convince me."

"Very well," said Rome. "It is very simple. It takes the form of a question."

"What question is that?"

"What is your purpose?" Rome asked.

Oronus pulled his head back. "My purpose?" he repeated. "Do you mean my occupation?"

"No," Rome said, "your purpose in life."

"I, I have no purpose," Oronus said. "I need none. I serve the Overmind, as do we all."

"Exactly! You serve the Overmind. You are not a person. You are just a puppet. Your directives could be for the better or the worse and you would never challenge them."

"Why would I challenge them?" asked Oronus, bristling. "By definition, whatever the Overmind wills is correct."

"The Overmind should serve the Vuduri, not the other way around. I can give you so many examples where the Overmind has erred," she said. "The Overmind is not infallible. It just thinks it is. However, I must agree: your original statement is correct. *You* have no real purpose. You are just a living machine serving the will of a power you do not understand."

"And you are any better?" Oronus said, his voice rising. "How can you have a purpose that is superior to serving the Overmind?"

"Because I am me," she announced. Because I am mandasurte, I have a purpose which has nothing to do with my occupation."

"So, enlighten me," Oronus said, tauntingly. "What is your purpose?"

"To live. To love. To be with Rei. To feel…every day," answered Rome proudly.

"That is not a purpose," Oronus said with disgust. "It is just a description of your current state. You betray your own argument. Your feelings get in the way. You cannot achieve anything with raw emotion dictating your actions."

"You do not know," Rome retorted. "You cannot know. You have only lived one way. I have lived both: connected and Cesdiud. The way I am now is the way I wish to be."

"I will challenge your position by stating the exact same thing. The way I am now is the way I wish to be as well. I cannot imagine living any other way."

"How would you know unless you tried both?"

Oronus shook his head. "This is not anything I will ever try. Therefore, we are at an impasse."

Rome sighed. "I know. You are wrong but I do understand your position. I was there once. We will never agree upon this," she said, flicking her hand at the tablet. "Why not just get to your questions?" She took a deep breath and let her face go blank.

"Thank you," replied Oronus. "I think we will do just that." He glanced down at his tablet and tapped a circle in the upper right. He looked up at Rome. "Why are you not on your way to Deucado? This is what we were told when your fellow crew members returned from Tabit."

Rome remained expressionless and spoke matter-of-factly, "We needed to come to Earth. Rei decided to let MINIMCOM tow his Ark to Deucado alone."

"Why did you need to come to Earth?"

Rome took a deep breath. "I became pregnant and we decided it would be better for me to give birth here."

"Why?" asked Oronus.

"Why did I become pregnant?"

"That is another matter altogether," Oronus replied. "Why did you decide it would be better to give birth on Earth?"

"I developed some complications," Rome said. Her lip started to quiver.

Oronus frowned. "Where are the MINIMCOM and the Ark now?"

"We separated from him near the star called Keid," replied Rome, almost in a monotone. "On his way to Deucado."

Oronus pushed the tablet toward Rome. "Show me," he said.

Rome looked down at the tablet. She saw dots representing Tabit, Keid, Deucado and Earth. She removed the stylus fastened to the side of the tablet and tapped the screen just to the right of Keid.

"Here," she said. "We released the Ark approximately here."

Oronus did not even look down but instead regarded Rome intently. "If this were the case, based upon the remaining distance, why did you not arrive here months earlier?" he asked.

Rome looked him in the eye. "The tug we were flying could not go at top speed," she replied flatly. "There was some flaw with the PPT generators."

"What was wrong with them?" Oronus asked. "Was it not something you could repair?"

"I do not know" Rome said. "For the first few weeks, everything was as expected but then the PPT projectors just started to wane. We were too far from MINIMCOM to ask for help and the nav-computer diagnostics could not really pinpoint a hardware issue. We did try but we were unable to get them back to optimal."

"Very well," Oronus said. "You said you were pregnant. Where is your baby?" he asked harshly.

Rome looked down at the table. Tears welled up in her eyes. She started to speak but her voice caught. She put her hands up to her eyes and began sobbing.

"Please, Rome…" Oronus said dismissively. "It is a simple question."

Rome fought back the tears and in a barely audible voice, she said, "Aason died at birth. Rei said he was stillborn."

"Do you retain the body?" Oronus asked coldly. "If so, where is it?"

"No," Rome answered, somewhat surprised at the question. She paused for a second. She thought furiously about Rei and his people and their curious customs. She knew what he would do, so she continued. "Rei had what he called a funeral for him. He made the baby a coffin and he set the body adrift in space." She started crying again.

This time, it was Oronus who seemed surprised. "Are you absolutely sure that is what happened?"

"Yes, I am sure," Rome said through her tears.

"That is a very strange thing to do. Did you think that was right?" Oronus asked. "To put the body in a coffin and put it into space?"

"No," Rome replied. "But Rei said it was the only way to honor his baby. I was so distraught. I did not fight him about it."

"I see," Oronus said. He paused for a moment. "It would appear that the Essessoni did many strange things."

Rome merely nodded. She sobbed softly, looking down at the floor.

"Take a moment to compose yourself," Oronus said, softening this time.

Rome took a deep breath. She looked up at Oronus with a steely expression in her eyes. "I am all right," she said.

"Good," Oronus said. "Now tell me about the Stareater. There is a recording on your ship that would indicate that the VIRUS units were successful in destroying it."

"Yes," she replied. "OMCOM told us that it was dead."

"How was it that OMCOM contacted you?"

"He developed a tightbeam using PPT modulation. He was able to target MINIMCOM's receiver and we conversed with him in real-time."

Oronus just shook his head. "Have you had any contact with OMCOM since that time?"

"No," Rome answered. "Just the one time."

Oronus nodded. He lifted his hand and waved it once. Rome turned to see that there was a quarter sphere attached where the ceiling met two of the walls. Based upon her knowledge of Vuduri standard procedure, she assumed there was a camera or other recording instruments contained there. The inner door opened and Grus came in, holding the door for Rei.

"Rei!" Rome said, getting up and running over to him. Rei put his arms around her and held her tightly. Rome heard a noise at the door and lifted her head up. Her eyes grew huge when Binoda entered the room.

"Aiee!" Rome shouted. "I cannot believe it! Mea!" She let go of Rei and grabbed her mother for dear life. Tears welled up in her eyes, yet again.

Her mother hugged her back. "Volhe," Binoda whispered holding her daughter. After a moment, Binoda put her hand under Rome's chin and lifted it up, peering into her eyes. "Cesdiud suits you well," Binoda said proudly.

Rome beamed at her all the while with tears streaming down her cheeks - but these were tears of pure joy.

"You have all seen her," Oronus said, finally interrupting the happy group. "Rome, do you have any last wishes before we carry out the sentence?"

"What sentence?" Rei snarled. "What about her trial?"

"There is no trial," Oronus said. "She has already been convicted."

# Chapter 10

"HOW CAN YOU CONVICT HER WITHOUT AT LEAST HEARING HER SIDE of the story?" Rei asked, trying to calm himself down. "What about the right to a fair trial?"

"Vuduri do not have trials," said Oronus.

"I thought you people were somehow supposed to be morally superior to my people," Rei protested. "At least we had that right back in my day. We had a whole bill of rights."

"It is not necessary," Oronus said. "I will demonstrate." The judge turned to look at Rome. "Rome, do you deny the charges?"

"Of course not," Rome said. "I fully acknowledge that I performed these actions and I would do it again if I had to."

"Very well," Oronus said. "Grus!" Grus took one step forward.

Rei moved over and put his body between Grus and Rome. Grus started to react then stopped. Rei turned his head back to Oronus. "What is the sentence?" he asked.

"For a capital crime such as this? The sentence is termination by evaporation, of course," replied Oronus without any hint of emotion.

Rome gasped. She put her arms around Rei from the back. The armed guard unslung his rifle and motioned it at Rei.

"No way!" Rei shouted. "They said I was the hero of Tabit. How could I be a hero unless what I did was the right thing to do?"

"You saved 80 Vuduri and quite possibly the Earth itself," answered Oronus. "You killed the Stareater. These are admirable things. Heroic things."

"So if I saved all these lives, how could I have done it without Rome?" Rei asked, his voice rising in fear. "How is what she did even a crime, anyway?"

"Have you had the opportunity to learn anything about our history?" asked Oronus.

"Yes," replied Rei. "Plenty."

"Then you know that a great war was fought over just such an issue."

"But there was no war here," Rei said. "All Rome did was enable OMCOM to kill the Stareater, not people. She didn't let

OMCOM into the Overmind club. She was the one who saved everybody's life."

"You are wrong. While your idea may have saved the lives of the Vuduri stationed at Tabit, Rome's actions have endangered all Vuduri for all time," pronounced Oronus, in a drone-like way. "You know about MASAL?"

Rei nodded.

Oronus continued, "Then you know after he created the 24$^{th}$ chromosome, the Overmind came into existence. MASAL was permitted to integrate into the Overmind. It was only after this happened that we found out that MASAL's goals were not in the best interests of the human race. This was our mistake, to enable a computer, an artificial intelligence, to have access to gravitic modulation. It let him grow without bound and it precipitated a war. All of our machines turned against us. It was the greatest loss of human life the world has ever seen, outside of your generation. What was done once can never be allowed to happen again. Computers are not meant to have access to unlimited resources. They must be kept in their place."

"But MASAL was analog," said Rei. "That was why he could merge with your Overmind in the first place. OMCOM is digital. He's completely incompatible. He could never integrate into your Overmind."

"It does not matter. Artificial intelligence does not have the necessary organic foundation to handle unlimited power. What Rome has enabled, Tasanceti, is an abomination and an anathema to all Vuduri. Her crime is absolute and her punishment has been preordained."

"Please step aside," Grus said, lowering his hand and patting a holster strapped to his leg. The holster contained some type of pistol. "You are finished here."

"We are not finished," Binoda said stepping forward. "Rome was authorized to perform this act by the Overmind at Tabit. That is the entity responsible for all of this, not her. She was just following orders."

"This is not true," Oronus said. "All of the individuals who returned from Tabit have been reintegrated into the Overmind of Earth. Not one of them has stated that Rome had permission."

"That is simply the position the Overmind expected," said Binoda. "Of course it is what they said. If I can produce a witness who will testify to the contrary, that she had permission, will you release her?"

"It is not possible," replied Oronus. "We have the collective consciousness of all the members of the Tabit expedition. We would know such a thing."

Rome whispered into Rei's ear. He looked up at the quarter sphere then turned to Oronus. "Is the T-suppression field still on? Are you connected right now to the Overmind?" He knew the answer because Rome said she could not connect to Aason.

Oronus looked at Grus who looked back at him.

"No," Oronus admitted. "But what does that have to do with anything?"

"If you are not connected at this moment," Binoda interrupted, "then you cannot say with absolute certainty that there is not one individual who would be willing to testify on Rome's behalf now that the request has been made."

"It is a simple matter of stepping outside that door," Oronus said, pointing to the doorway. "I would reconnect and then I would know."

"Then do so," Binoda said. "And call Commander Ursay. Have him come here immediately."

"It is not necessary for him to come here," Oronus said. "I would know his testimony right away."

"Do you see these two mandasurte here," Binoda said, indicating Rei and Rome. "How can they know what he says? They will only have your word for it."

"My word is sufficient," Oronus said. "Vuduri do not lie."

"Ha!" Rei exclaimed. "Of course you do."

"We do not," replied Oronus calmly even as his face tightened.

"Yes, you do," Rei said, scoffing at the statement. "There are two kinds of lies. There are the kinds that you say and there are things that you do not say. Are you even pretending that Vuduri never keep secrets from one another?"

Oronus glared at Rei and did not speak for a moment. He looked up at the quarter sphere in the corner of the room. "Get me Ursay," he said finally.

# Chapter 11

IT TOOK LESS THAN AN HOUR TO LOCATE AND TRANSPORT Commander Ursay from his home to the north, near what had been called Amarante. In the mean-time, several chairs were brought in and arranged with Rei, Rome and Binoda on the left and Grus sitting to the right. Oronus remained behind the desk the entire time. One other chair, empty at the moment, was placed in the middle, directly in front of Oronus.

Ursay walked into the room and immediately put his hands on his head. To Rei, he looked like he had aged substantially since the last time they saw him, just a year ago. Where there had been just a hint of gray around his temples, his hair was mostly gray now and thinning a bit at the crown. There were light creases in his face as if he had been in the sun much too long.

"What is this place?" Ursay inquired. "Why am I no longer connected?"

"This room is under continuous T-suppression," Oronus said.

"Why?" Ursay asked, walking forward. He glanced over and saw Rei and Rome. He flashed them a faint smile before sitting down in the vacant chair."

"As you already know, the Overmind wishes it," said Oronus. "That should be sufficient."

"I do not know," Ursay replied. "The reason was kept hidden."

Oronus took a deep breath but said nothing.

"Tell me why I am here," demanded Ursay.

"Rome has been convicted of the most serious of crimes. That of giving Tasanceti to a computer. This is the most heinous act that can be committed."

"I know this," replied Ursay. "You know this. This explains nothing."

"These people claim that the Overmind of Tabit, through you as its agent, gave her permission and therefore sanctioned this action."

"We did no such thing," Ursay said. "Rome acted of her own volition."

"Thank you," Oronus replied. "Now. Are you satisfied?" Oronus directed to Rei.

"No!" Rei said, standing up. He walked over to Commander Ursay. "I need to ask Ursay some questions."

"Very well," Oronus said, exhaustedly. "You may."

Rei regarded Ursay. "You remember the events leading up to this so-called crime, right?"

"Yes, of course," Ursay stated. "You were there as well."

"Right," Rei replied. "I was there. I was there when you told Rome that no Vuduri could ever be part of the unleashing."

"Yes," said the older man. "Rome pointed out that she was Cesdiud and therefore mandasurte so she could do it."

"What did you do at that point?"

"I told her and you to find another way. That there had to be another solution."

"And what did we come up with? All of us together?"

"Nothing, really," said Ursay. "There did not appear to be another solution at the time."

"So Rome asked you to let her do it. She said if it bothered you, you could just ignore her. In fact, she said 'let me do it and you will have no part in this,' right?"

"Yes," Ursay replied.

"So when she said let me do it…how is that not asking your permission? You had every opportunity to stop her. And you did not."

"She would have done it anyway," Ursay said.

"Nonetheless, she said to you let me do this and you answered what?" Rei shot back.

Ursay did not speak for a moment. He closed his eyes as if to recall the incident. Suddenly he snapped his eyes open. "I instructed her to do what she must."

"And you were the commander of the station," Rei followed with too much vigor. "She was compelled to follow your orders, even though she was mandasurte. I even called you out on it. This was before Rome did anything. I pointed out to you that you were about to have Rome commit a crime. *You!*" Rei said, pointing right at Ursay. "I told you that was the same as you giving her the OK. And you said what?"

"At the time, I told you that you were correct," answered Ursay.

Rei turned to Oronus. "There. He said it. He told her to do it and she was just following orders. If you convict her of this crime, then you have to convict her superiors that gave the order. Which means Ursay and every person that was part of the Overmind of Tabit."

"That would be impractical," sputtered Oronus. "They have been reintegrated. We would have to indict every Vuduri on Earth."

"Then let her go," Binoda called out, standing abruptly. "You have your proof. We are all guilty of the same crime. And it is only a crime if our society says it is. Since Rome had permission of every Vuduri on Earth there was no crime."

"You are forgetting one thing," Ursay interrupted.

"What is that?" Rei asked.

"I warned you that your view of this was strictly from your perspective. I told you that no Vuduri, no one connected to the Overmind could take part in that activity. I told you that if Rome performed the act of her own volition, she would be responsible for the consequences, her and her alone. Not us."

"Those are just words," Rei said with disgust. He pointed to Ursay. "I told you before and I'll tell you again. You people are lunatics and hypocrites."

Ursay shrugged this off. "Nonetheless," he said, "I disavowed any association with the action prior to it being executed."

"Did you forbid her then?" Rei asked.

"Obviously not," replied Ursay.

"Yet you said Rome did this of her own volition."

"Yes," Ursay responded.

"If converting memrons to PPT modulation was so horrible, so wrong," Rei asked. "Why even have a system that was capable of such action?"

"There were interlocks that should have prevented it. They needed willful actions to be overridden," Ursay said. "No Vuduri would ever do that. Therefore there was no need to build in a higher level of protection."

"No Vuduri," Rei answered back. "But an independent mandasurte?"

"Yes, mandasurte," Ursay replied. "Her," he said, pointing to Rome."

"How did she get that way? How did she come to be mandasurte, autonomous?"

"She was Cesdiud. You know this."

"Of course I know it," Rei said. "But why did you do it? Why the Cesdiud?"

Ursay took a deep breath. He looked legitimately hurt. Finally, he answered. "Because of you," he said sadly. "We thought her association with you would taint our perspective."

"You picked Rome to interact with me because of her heritage. She was disposable right from the start."

"Yes, to this I can agree. We knew she could be jettisoned with the least impact on our Overmind."

Binoda made a hissing noise but said nothing.

"Your loss, my gain," Rei said snidely. "Getting back to her Cesdiud, Who decided she had too much contact with me? Whose brilliant idea was that? Was it the Overmind that figured that out?" he asked.

Ursay thought for a minute. "Actually, it was OMCOM that called it to our attention," Ursay said sheepishly.

"And you do not think he had his own motives for pointing that out?" Rei asked angrily.

"I suppose he did, but we agreed with his reasoning at the time."

"I am going to tell you why she was cast out," Rei spat the words. "She was cast out for the exact reason that she could act autonomously so she could perform the override that was necessary to kill the Stareater. Hell, you sanctified the action. You even sent Signola along to help her. Right?"

"Yes," Ursay said quietly. "But Signola did nothing wrong. He never actually performed the override."

Rei didn't answer for a minute. He gazed off into space, replaying the incident in his mind for the fortieth time. Suddenly, he snapped his fingers. "I got it!" he said.

"Got what?" Oronus asked.

Rei turned back to Ursay. "I just remembered your exact last words to Rome before she left to do it. Do you?"

"Yes," replied Ursay.

"So tell Oronus what your last three words to her were exactly."

Ursay took a deep breath. "My last three words were, 'You may proceed.'"

Rei wheeled in place to look right at Oronus. "If that isn't permission, I don't know what is." He looked over at his wife. Strangely, she was smiling. He turned back to Oronus. "Rome was set up. She was selected for this job right from the start. She was cast out so she could perform this action. She was given permission and therefore commanded by the Overmind. The results of her actions are lauded by you and all the Vuduri. There is no crime. SO LET HER GO."

He turned back to Ursay and in a lower voice said, "Please tell him the truth."

Ursay stared up at Rei for the longest time. He glanced over at Rome then stood up.

"I am changing my testimony," he said to Oronus. "I am going on record as stating that the Overmind of Tabit gave Rome permission, and in fact ordered her to perform these actions. Upon further reflection, I now concur that we are as culpable and therefore as guilty as Rome. If you must convict her of this crime and still choose to execute her, you will have to execute me and by extension every Vuduri on the planet."

Oronus glanced over at Grus who had given up and sat completely helpless. Oronus looked up at the quarter sphere in the corner and said, "That is ridiculous. We cannot execute ourselves." He leaned back in his chair and took a deep breath. He folded his hands together, resting them on his stomach, staring down at them.

Finally, he lifted his head and spoke. "I cannot set aside the verdict. Rome still performed the actions. The crime stands. The only thing I can do is commute the sentence."

"To what?" Rei asked.

"Banishment," Oronus replied. "Rome must be isolated from all Vuduri and anything resembling synthesizer technology. She must never be allowed to carry out any such acts again."

"What would the point be?" Rei asked. "You already have the VIRUS units. She would not need to ever do such a thing again. Nobody does."

"Incorrect," said Oronus. "We do not have the VIRUS units."

"What do you mean?" Rome asked, rising in her seat.

"When we arrived on Earth, the Overmind ordered them destroyed," replied Ursay.

"You what?!" Rei shouted. "How are you going to stop the Stareater when it gets here?"

"We do not know," Oronus said. "Unless we come up with an alternative, our current plan is to abandon the Earth. We are building some transports, ironically, similar to your Arks, to move a percentage of the population to another star system. Beyond that, we are still working on finding another technology to perform the same function as the VIRUS units but we are not hopeful."

"And what if Asdrale Cimatir arrives tomorrow?" Rome asked. "What will you do?"

"We can only hope that does not occur," replied Oronus. "Our last projections based upon data returned from Tabit indicate we should have well over one year left. Currently, we believe we can save as much as ten percent of the population, although that may be optimistic."

Rei looked at Rome then back at Oronus.

"Why not deploy VIRUS units at least until you come up with your magical alternative?" Rei asked. "Did you not save any of them?"

"No," replied Ursay sadly.

Rei looked back at him. "What if I could..."

Rome jumped up and shouted "No!" Rei shut up immediately.

"What is the problem?" asked Oronus. "Rei, continue. What if you could what?"

Rome interrupted. "Whatever Rei was going to offer, I will not allow him," Rome said. "This is your problem now, not ours. We have done our best. Are we free to go?"

"No, you are not," Oronus replied. "There are the conditions of your release."

"And what are those?"

"You must retire to a place where there is no molecular synthesis equipment nor any type of fabrication or computing facilities. You must be exiled and kept isolated from all Vuduri and all Vuduri technology."

"What about the mandasurte?" Binoda asked. "Can she remain among them?"

"As long as it is a community that has none of the technology mentioned," Oronus said.

"I have a place," Binoda offered.

"Where?" said Oronus.

"What about Ylea, on Mowei?" Binoda asked.

"Mowei…Maui?" asked Rei, "Hawaii?"

Binoda nodded and continued, "Yes, Havei. That is where Rome's father was born and raised. It is a mandasurte community. Rome still has family there. Portions of it are very primitive and have none of the technological components you insist she stay away from."

Oronus looked up at the quarter sphere then down at his tablet. "That is acceptable," he said.

Binoda looked at Rome who nodded and said, "That is fine."

"Then it is agreed," said Binoda.

"Uh, what about our Flying House?" Rei asked. "Do we get to keep it?"

"Of course not," replied Oronus dismissively. "It has the very equipment onboard that we are trying to keep Rome away from."

"What about our stuff?" Rei asked.

"To what are you referring?"

"All of our stuff," Rei replied. "Our things, our belongings. We have stuff on the ship."

"Rome is to be banished immediately," answered Oronus. "We do not want to spend any time unloading and transferring your belongings."

"I have an idea," Rei said. "How about you fly us there in that ship? That way, we can unload it when we get there and then you can take it away."

"Fair enough," replied Oronus.

"So, we have an agreement?" Rei asked.

"Yes. The banishment is to begin now," announced Oronus. He signaled to the quarter sphere in the corner of the ceiling. "Grus, accompany them to their spacecraft, please. It is already on its way."

Rome moved around to Rei. She kissed him and hugged him.

"I did not know you were such a good..." Rome paused, trying to recollect the word. "Yes, 'lawyer,' I think that is the term you use," she said. Rei grinned. "I think I will keep you," she said happily.

"Try and get rid of me," Rei said with a smile and they started to walk out.

"Binoda," Oronus called out to her. "You may not accompany them to Ylea. Rome must not have contact with any Vuduri after today."

Binoda shook her head. "I am going with them. From this moment forward, I am no longer connected. I have just rendered myself Cesdiud. I am mandasurte now."

"Mea!" Rome said in horror. "You cannot."

"It is already done," replied Binoda grimly. "I no longer have any use for the Overmind."

"No, no, no," Rome said. Her shoulders slumped. "You need to go back."

Grus ignored Rome's outburst and hustled them out of the courtroom. As soon as they were outside the door, Rome's link to Aason was reestablished.

"*Mother!*" Aason said. "*I missed you. Where have you been? Where are you now?*"

"*We are here, baby,*" Rome replied sadly.

"*Are you all right?*"

"*Yes. We are leaving this place and going somewhere where we can be together.*"

"*I would very much like that. When can I be with you?*"

"*Soon, baby, very soon,*" replied Rome. "*Let me attend to our affairs and I will let you know. There has been a change in plans. I will have MINIMCOM bring you to us when the time is right.*"

"*I cannot wait, Mother.*"

"*Me neither,*" Rome said and she narrowed the connection to a tiny thread.

Grus and two other soldiers along with Ursay accompanied them outside. They did not have to wait long until the tug known as the Flying House flew overhead and settled down in the courtyard. The cargo door raised and the ramp lowered. Rome turned to Ursay.

"Thank you for all you have done," she said.

"There is no reason to thank me. The truth is the truth," replied Ursay with the defocused look of someone who was attending to the Overmind. "Good luck in your future endeavors," he said to Rei and Rome.

"Thank you," Rome replied. "I hope you will come visit us some time."

"I do not think that will be permitted," Ursay said. "Goodbye." With that he turned and walked away.

"Business as usual," Rei muttered to Rome. He held her hand and together they walked up the ramp followed by Binoda and Grus. As soon as the cargo compartment was sealed, the tug rose up in the air and they were on their way.

# Chapter 12

THE SHIP HEADED WEST, OVER THE ATLANTIC, EVENTUALLY traveling at four times the speed of sound. After an hour of sitting around and doing nothing, Binoda stood up and wandered about, inspecting the artwork mounted in various spots around the room.

"Whose handiwork?" she asked in Vuduri.

"It is mine, Mea," Rome replied.

"How did you learn to craft these works?"

"I learned many things once I was Cesdiud. I learned about art, beauty, music, Rei's history. As you can imagine, we had much time."

"Stuck in this ship for a year? I should say so."

"It was not bad." Rome looked at Grus. "We have time. May I show my mother around?"

"No," Grus replied gruffly. "We insist you remain within visual contact at all times."

"Then you accompany us," Rome said, standing up.

Grus sighed and stood up. "Please remain here," he said to Rei.

Rei just shrugged. "Where am I going to go?" he asked, hands held outward.

Grus shook his head. "Proceed," he said to the two women and the three of them left the room. Rome took Grus and her mother down the hallway toward the very back of the ship. "This was our recycling facility," she said, pointing to the right. "Rei insisted we launder rather than synthesize clothes all the time so he built me what he called a washing machine."

Binoda looked puzzled. "That seems so inefficient on a space voyage," she said.

"Yes," Rome said. "Many of Rei's customs seem strange to me but for some things, I let him have his own way."

"I understand. Your father also had some peculiar ideas," Binoda replied somewhat sadly. They turned and walked part way back up the hall. Rome pointed to her left. "In that room is storage and our life support, molecular sequencers and more."

Grus took one step forward and placed his hand on the middle of the door.

72

"Do not worry," Rome said. "I will not go in there." As if to demonstrate her good behavior, she spun in place in an attempt at drama. She pointed to the door to Binoda's left. They moved forward and entered the doorway into their bedroom.

Binoda looked around. She spotted the onyx case that contained the espansors. She walked over and picked it up and turned toward Rome, holding it out. Rome nodded. Binoda smiled and placed the case back on the dresser. After taking one more look, Binoda said, "It is very nice, Rome."

"Thank you, Mea," she said. "Come."

Rome led them back into the hallway and toward the front into their little galley. She showed Binoda the oven next to the food synthesizers and the food preparation area. She pointed to the elaborate rack of spices, mounted on the galley wall.

"Rei has taught me so many things about food," she stated. "As you know, the Vuduri do not care about such things. But, what we ate here...?" She stopped speaking and looked up to the corner of the room. "I can only describe it using the English word Rei taught me: heavenly," she said finally.

"I can see that you enjoyed it," Binoda said, pointing her finger at Rome's waist. "There is now more of my daughter to love than before you left."

Rome blushed. "Yes, Mea, I know," she said. "When we are settled, I plan to reduce my weight back to its optimal. The gravity on Earth will help me with my exercises, make them more effective."

"It is all right," Binoda said. "You look very healthy," she said. Then, after a moment, she added, "And happy. Your new life agrees with you."

"Yes, it does, Mea," Rome said. "I could not ask for a more wonderful partner. I cannot even tell you how many hours we spent here, laughing, playing games. We never grew tired of each other, not once, during the entire trip."

Binoda looked around, trying to envision that. She stopped and stared at the dining table for a moment. "Why are there three chairs?" she asked Rome, pointing at the table.

"What?" Rome said, her eyes widening. She took a deep breath. They had purposefully destroyed Aason's high chair. The thought never occurred to them to destroy Fridone's.

"Eh, that is just the way we made it," Rome replied finally. "The galley was built with two chairs. There came a time when we wanted another." Subtly, she shook her head and dragged her mother out of the room.

Binoda asked. "What if you wanted to be alone? Where would you go?"

"It was not like that," Rome said. "It was not really taxing. Rei and I enjoyed each other's company so much that the time passed very quickly. If I was painting and needed to be alone, Rei would go up to the cockpit or the galley. Sometimes, when he was in the studio, recording his oral history, he would want to be alone as well. I would go lie down in the bedroom or do laundry. We were fine. But mostly we did not really want to be apart from one another."

"I was that way with your father," Binoda said. "I never got enough time with him." Her voice trailed off.

Rome put her arm around her mother. "Come, Mea," she said.

"No. It is enough," said Grus. "Please go back to the living area for the remainder of the journey."

Rome and Binoda complied. When they got back to the room that doubled as a studio, Rei was sitting at the workstation.

"What are you doing?" Grus asked.

"I was hooking into the nav-system. Do you care?"

"I suppose not," Grus said wearily.

"Thanks," Rei said in English. He activated the ventral cameras just as they passed over the isthmus of Panama. In front of them lay the vast expanse of the Pacific with a few wisps of whitecaps. The instruments indicated they were about 12 kilometers up. Rei adjusted some filters. A polarizer removed the glare and rippling from the waves and made the water look completely transparent. From this height, Rei was able to see detail along the ocean bottom clearly enough to make out some of its topology. He could see crevices, channels and even some peaks that looked like underwater mountains. If you ignored the fact that it was deep blue, some of it even reminded Rei of the surface of the moon.

After a bit, on the horizon, a landmass appeared that Rei guessed was the Big Island of Hawaii. As they got closer, he became certain of it. Their craft banked northward and flew directly over the peaks of Kilauea and the even taller Mauna Loa. To his right was the older, rounder shape of Mauna Kea. It did not take long until they passed back out over the ocean. Directly ahead was the peculiar arrowhead-shaped island of Maui. There were heavy clouds on the northern side of the island where the sea breezes met the mountain peaking in the middle of the island. They flew over the southern side and Rei could see the mammoth crater of Haleakala, which he had learned about as a child.

Lower and lower they flew, nearing the western edge of the larger portion of the island, flying over a wide beach and a stand of trees, coming to a halt over a smaller, crescent-shaped beach. The ship descended until it came to rest in the sand.

The assembled group started to stand but Grus held up his hand. "Please remain here," he said. "I must survey the area first." He returned a few minutes later. "There is an abandoned dwelling very near here," he said. "You may take that as your shelter for the time being."

Grus made a waving motion to Rei. "The pilots will help you gather your belongings. We will wait for you outside," he said. He accompanied the two women through the hallway and down the cargo ramp.

Rei crossed over into the bedroom and was surprised to see some empty satchels sitting on the bed. He shrugged and gathered up their clothing, their toiletries and most importantly, the bands. It seemed like forever since he and Rome had last used them to commingle their minds. He handed one of the satchels to a pilot then returned to the living area to gather up Rome's artwork and her paint supplies. He also grabbed his solid-state music slab which he had rescued from the Ark along with a datacube filled with MINIMCOM's original works. He didn't know when he would ever get a chance to play them again but after all the effort they had made to accumulate the collection, he was not going to just abandon it. Looking around, he saw nothing else of value. He exited and joined Rome and Binoda at the base of the ramp.

Grus addressed the three of them. "Your dwelling is just up that trail," he said, pointing toward a rocky path leading away from the beach. He beckoned to Rome who took one step closer to him. "Please extend your wrist," he asked her.

"Why?" Rome inquired.

"For this." Grus reached into his pocket and removed a thin silver bracelet. He looked at Rome's outstretched arm for a moment, staring at the ring on her finger. He shrugged then snapped the bracelet around her wrist. Where there had been an opening, the metal sealed forming a smooth finish which was now seamless.

"This is a tracking bracelet," he said. "It is required because you are mandasurte. The conditions of your release are that you are to remain on or about this island. Please make no attempt to contact anyone off island and please do not try to access any technology. The very fact that you remain alive is a gift. Always remember that."

"I will," Rome said solemnly. "Thank you."

Grus defocused and then turned to look at Rei. "While you are a hero, your continued association with a convicted criminal makes you unwelcome within the Vuduri world. I would ask that you remain here as well."

"You do realize that you just transported me to paradise with the woman I love?" Rei said in English. "Why would I want to leave?"

Grus did not answer. He looked at Binoda. "The same punishment goes for you as well."

"It is not a punishment, I assure you," Binoda said.

"No matter," Grus replied. "Goodbye." With that, he turned and walked up the ramp.

Rome reached over and took Rei's hand as the cargo ramp retracted and the hatch lowered. The Flying House, their home for the last year and more, rose up into the air and began to move forward toward the sun, which was very low in the sky. The tug banked over the ocean coming all the way around then flew back directly overhead, all the while heading upwards. As their former craft/home arose high in the sky, a tear came to Rome's eye which she wiped with her free hand. "I will miss it," she said.

"Me too," Rei replied. They watched as the Flying House became smaller and smaller until finally it disappeared. They stared at the darkening sky and low-lying white clouds for a long while. Finally, Rome squeezed Rei's hand to get his attention. Rei turned to her.

"Now we get to do our work," she said.

# Chapter 13

Binoda stared at her daughter, completely confused. "What work?" she asked. "Should we not go to the shelter?"

"We will, Mea" Rome replied, "but we must remain here for a short while. I promise to fill you in on all the details. For now, let me summarize. You will recall my assignment and circumstance at the observation station within the Tabit star system."

"Yes, of course," her mother answered. "You covered that in your letter to me. It was very touching. You are a good writer, Rome."

"Thank you, Mea, but I simply told the truth."

"Still, you were very kind to send it. Continue."

Rome pointed upward. "After I was Cesdiud, we had figured out that it was a giant thing, Asdrale Cimatir, which was consuming stars. Rei invented the technique which I had to implement to kill it."

"I understood that from the crew that returned from Tabit as well as the comments Oronus made," said Binoda.

"Yes, but you understand I had no choice. As Rei pointed out, they set me up so that I could do what I had to do without culpability."

"She was their scapegoat," Rei threw in.

"That is just like the Overmind," said Binoda. "Go on."

"Well, before we left, they gave us *two* tugs, the Flying House and another ship to tow Rei's Ark to Deucado. The Flying House is the ship that they just took away."

"What happened to the other tug?" Binoda asked.

"It's hard to explain," Rei chimed in.

"Try," Binoda commanded.

Rome shivered and then her smile brightened. "I will do better than that, Mea," she said, touching her temple. "Let us watch the sunset."

"We can do that another time, Rome," said Binoda, impatiently. "Please enlighten me."

Rei touched his temple as well.

"You really want to see the sunset," Rei added. "Everything will become clear."

Binoda looked even more confused but gave up arguing. The beach they were on was made of pure white sand, almost like flour. The area was somewhat secluded by large boulders on the far ends and a stand of palm trees all around them. The beach overlooked the Pacific which stretched as far as the eye could see.

As the sun went down, the beautiful colors playing among the low-lying clouds made for a spectacular view. A gentle breeze brought the ubiquitous smell of jasmine and plumeria wafting over them. Rei stood with his arm around Rome just reveling in the peace of their current situation. The sunset was magnificent, as it always is in Hawaii, but Binoda seemed distracted and unimpressed. They even had the opportunity to see a tiny green flash on the top of the sun just before it set.

As the glowing shards of light waned, Binoda could no longer control her impatience. "I understand nothing better," she said to Rome. "It is a sunset. I have seen them before."

"Not like this one," Rome replied, pointing over the ocean.

Binoda turned to look at where Rome was pointing. She was indicating exactly where the sun had been as the orb disappeared below the horizon. Binoda looked and saw that the air began shimmering, somewhat like one would see just before a mirage appeared in the desert. A ghostly presence sparkled then disappeared and then reappeared. The giant ball of diffraction drifted in from the ocean and settled on the beach, just to the south.

Binoda stared at it, trying to understand what her eyes were telling her. In front of her, four deep depressions appeared in the sand. A whining, jet-enginey kind of sound filled the air then died off. In front of her, a cavity appeared 10 feet up, right in the middle of the air.

"This is your other ship?" Binoda asked. "It is a hole in the air. What is this?"

"Just watch, Mea," Rome said with a broad smile on her face.

As Binoda peered into the hole, a gray, metallic-looking ramp became visible and lowered until it came to rest in the sand. Something stirring was stirring at the back of the compartment. A robed figure moved forward. When the individual got to the top of the ramp, he stopped and stood there quietly.

"Who is that?" Binoda asked, turning to Rome.

Rome just smiled as Rei squeezed her tighter. She tilted her head indicating the figure within the ship. Binoda turned back to look at man at the top of the ramp, adjusting her vision to telescopic.

"No," she breathed, plaintively, not able to tear her eyes away. "It cannot be."

"It is, Mea," Rome exclaimed tearfully. "It is. Go to him."

"Fridone!" Binoda shouted and sprinted up the ramp to meet her husband at the top. She kissed him and hugged him and kissed him and hugged him. She was overwhelmed. It was a long time before she was able to speak coherently.

"Oh, husband," she said finally. "Look at you. Your hair! So gray!" Binoda sighed and whispered, "I have missed you so much." She grabbed his cheeks with her hands and touched her forehead to his, closing her eyes.

"My beautiful Binoda," Fridone said. "I have missed you more."

"That is not possible," she said, opening her eyes again. "How did this happen?"

"You may thank your resourceful daughter," Fridone said, pointing back down at Rome, standing on the beach. "She saved me. She saved my world and she is here to save this one as well."

"Your world?" his wife asked, somewhat perplexed. "This is your world." Binoda paused for a second. "Where were you, anyway?"

"The Onsiras stole me away from here," Fridone said, somewhat with disgust. "They imprisoned me."

"Imprisoned? And who are the Onsiras? I do not understand."

"You will. We will explain everything. For now, all you need to know is that I am free and we can be together again."

"I cannot believe it," Binoda exclaimed. "This is the best moment of my life."

Rome flexed her shoulders so Rei released her. She jogged up the ramp to join the reunited couple. "There is more, Mea," she said.

"More?" replied Binoda, confused. She looked at Fridone who smiled and merely shrugged.

"Yes," Rome answered. "Wait here." She brushed past them and disappeared inside the ship.

"I do not understand any of this," Binoda said. "I see a very large inside but there is no outside. We are in the middle of the air with nothing holding us up."

Rei approached and climbed the ramp to the top. "This is the other tug that Rome mentioned. His name is MINIMCOM," he said.

"A MINIMCOM is a computer," answered Binoda. "This is a vehicle, invisible or not."

"Yes and yes," Rei replied. "MINIMCOM has been through a lot but he started out as a computer. Now he is a ship and a computer and much, much more."

"Why could I not see it as it approached?" Binoda asked. "Is this magic?"

"Not magic, my dear Binoda," Fridone said, "MINIMCOM is just very clever."

"Yes, very clever," Rome called out from the far end of the cargo compartment. Binoda turned to see her daughter walk toward them cradling a bundle of blankets in her arms. "I have something to show you," Rome said.

"What is this you have brought me?" Binoda asked.

Rome pulled back the blanket, revealing the baby inside. "This is your grandson, Aason!"

Binoda's eyes grew wide. Tears welled up in her eyes again. "A grandson? Rome!"

She put out her arms and Rome handed her the baby boy. Instinctively, Binoda held him and rocked him and began swaying her hips side to side as had humans for the last million years. She stared down at his angelic face. Aason stretched his mouth in what almost looked like a smile then slowly, with agonizing care, turned his head toward Rome. Even at this young age, he was exceptionally strong and exceptionally coordinated, even for a Vuduri. Then he turned back to Binoda, closed his eyes and gave a deep sigh.

81

Rome said, "He is glad to meet you, Mea. He says hello."

Binoda shook her head, holding the baby out to see. "What do you mean?"

"Aason and I are connected," her daughter answered. She reached over and took the baby back, placing him close to her heart.

"How is this possible?" Binoda asked. "You were Cesdiud. I am Cesdiud. I cannot hear him."

"I was reconnected on Deucado," Rome replied, "as was Aason."

"Deucado?" Rome's mother gasped. "How were you there? Then how are you here?"

"Let us go find our lodgings," Rome offered. "Then we can begin fitting the pieces of this puzzle together for you."

"I would very much like that," said Binoda. She turned and took two steps down the ramp. She looked over her shoulder and noticed that nobody was following her.

"What?" she asked.

"I must be very careful," said Fridone.

"Why?" asked Binoda, coming back up the ramp.

Rome answered for him. "Beo is not supposed to be here and they do not know I have a baby."

"How are you going to hide them?" Binoda asked.

"Watch," Rome said and she handed the baby back to her father. He pulled his cloak around himself, covering Aason in the process. He lowered his hand along the edge of the cloak and disappeared.

"What?" Binoda exclaimed in shock. "What happened to him?"

"I am right here," Fridone answered, seemingly from thin air.

"More magic?" Binoda remarked. "You certainly seemed to have mastered this, this invisibility mechanism."

"Actually, this was a present from the Deucadons," Rei said. "They are a group of my people who got stranded on Deucado 500 years ago. They still live there."

"I do not understand anything," Binoda harrumphed. "You will have to start from the beginning. What is going on?"

"Mea, let us go find our shelter and I will explain all. I promise."

"Very well," Binoda answered resignedly.

The visible three and the invisible two walked down to the base of the ramp. Binoda turned back and looked up. She saw the ramp and the cavity but could not see anything else. She walked over to where she thought the ship should be and passed her hand over the spot. She could feel nothing.

"Is it possible to turn this shield off?" Binoda asked. "Can I see the vehicle?"

Rei came up to stand beside her. "MINIMCOM will let you see him but it can only be for a second," he said. "He is not supposed to be here either."

Rei closed his eyes then opened them again.

Taking his cue, MINIMCOM dropped the cloak long enough for Binoda to see a huge black cargo ship with a flowing, sleek shape bristling with a whole battery of PPT generators and plasma engines, mounted on the airfoils.

Rei looked at his friend who was also a ship. In no way did MINIMCOM resemble the original shuttle that was his starting point. Beyond that, something else stood out. MINIMCOM looked totally different on the outside from even when Rei had seen him last.

*"What gives?"* Rei thought to MINIMCOM.

*"Whatever do you mean?"* replied MINIMCOM ever so innocently.

*"You're all decorated with doodads and spirals. You didn't have them before."* Rei thought.

*"Oh those,"* stated MINIMCOM. *"I determined that I would have better aerodynamic control if I had a reliable and steady flow of turbulence within my air stream when I was in the atmosphere. The somewhat symmetrical nature of the designs was an attempt, only slightly successful, to inversely impress the turbulence, to cancel it, so that the net effect was still air, even though I gained the immediate advantage of microturbulence."*

*"Well, they're pretty sharp, if you ask me,"* Rei said, knowing MINIMCOM was full of baloney.

*"Why thank you,"* MINIMCOM said then he winked out.

"Just like that?" Binoda asked. "How is this possible?"

"Mea," Rome called out to them. "Let us go inside so that Beo and Aason can come out. We will explain it to you as I promised."

Binoda nodded and joined her daughter. They picked up a few of the items left on the beach, leaving the heavier satchels for Rei.

Rei glanced over at the suitcases then back to the empty air where MINIMCOM was located. He said in his head, *"You know you're pretty sleek, dude. Your entrance and exits are getting more impressive every time."*

`"I aim to please,"` replied MINIMCOM.

*"You sure do! OK, I'll be back later,"* Rei said and he turned to walk away.

He hadn't even taken two steps when MINIMCOM interrupted him.

`"Before you leave, I need you to come up to my cockpit."`

*"Why?"* Rei asked in his mind.

`"I have something for you."`

*"All right,"* Rei thought. Then out loud, he shouted, "Romey, I'll catch up to you in a minute. MINIMCOM has something to show me."

"Very well," Rome called back as she led her parents up the rocky path. "We will go find our lodgings."

Rei climbed up the ramp and into the cargo hold of MINIMCOM. As he looked around, he said out loud, "I think you need to go on a diet."

`"Why?"` MINIMCOM asked through a grille.

"You sure are a lot bigger than you used to be, even than before," Rei said with a smile on his face. "Kind of a wide load now if you know what I mean."

`"The better to serve you,"` MINIMCOM replied with just a hint of sarcasm in his voice. `"My constructors have been busy. Now please come forward."`

"OK," Rei said as he entered the cockpit. "What've you got?"

A panel opened and with the diffuse glow of backlighting, Rei could see a shape within. "What is it?" he asked.

`"Take it,"` MINIMCOM said.

Rei reached in and removed a pouch that looked somewhat like leather. Along its top edges, there was a drawstring. Rei teased the opening apart and looked inside. All he saw was a dark grayish substance, reminiscent of talcum powder. Sprinkled throughout were larger, black dots that had a metallic sheen to them. Rei reached in and felt around but there was nothing remarkable about it. The substance felt very light, not gritty like sand. He drew the string closed again and placed it on the opened door in front of him.

"What's in here?" he asked, "ground up aerogel?"

`"They are a gift from OMCOM. They are a special type of VIRUS units, taken and modified from my skin."`

"What?!" Rei said, leaping up. Instinctively, he wiped his hand on his pants but in his heart, he knew it was not going to matter. "What the hell?"

`"It is all right,"` MINIMCOM said with a mechanical chuckle. `"You are safe. They are currently dormant. These particular VIRUS units will not digest organic matter."`

Rei sank down into the pilot's chair. "Why are you giving them to me?" he asked.

`"OMCOM said he computed multiple scenarios whereupon you would require them. I have modified them according to his specifications."`

"How are they modified?"

`"These are super VIRUS units, weaponized. They reproduce in seconds. They can be assigned specific tasks. They will work autonomously or as an integrated cluster. Their oxygen sensor has been disabled so they can work in an atmosphere if required."`

Rei's eyes widened. "You mean they can destroy the Earth?"

`"In theory, yes. In practice, no. As I said, these particular units will not ingest organic matter. They are strictly limited to metals or minerals. The larger ones…"`

"The black ones?" Rei interrupted.

`"Yes, the black ones. You may call them queens. They will control the other units. The queens are completely under your control. You decide when they are active and when they are dormant."`

"Me?" Rei said. "I don't get it."

`"They are equipped with receivers for your 'cellphone' link. They answer to you. You give them an assignment and they will follow it."`

"Just me? How about Rome?"

`"Yes, they would answer to Rome as well,"` replied MINIMCOM.

Rei looked down at the pouch, sitting within the compartment. He stared at it for a while, his mind racing. "Are you going to tell me when and where I'm supposed to use them?"

"I cannot. OMCOM did not share that specific information with me."

"Great. Say I do use them, what if they mutate?"

"These particular units will not mutate, I assure you."

"How can you know? OMCOM's did."

"I have implemented a checksum code. If the unit reproduces and the checksum does not match, the unit will shut down."

"Hold on a minute," Rei said. "If you were able to figure out how to suppress mutations, how come OMCOM didn't. I mean, OMCOM is way smarter than you, no offense intended."

"None taken."

"So then why didn't he prevent them, too?" Rei asked."

"I suppose I will let you in on a little secret."

"What?"

"I did not actually design the checksum code. It was already built into the programming in the original VIRUS units. There was a conditional branch that skipped over the algorithm under certain circumstances. I simply removed the branch so that the checksum is always executed."

"What?" Rei exclaimed. "You've got to be kidding me. That means..." Rei's voice failed him. He took a deep breath to regain control then spoke again. "That means OMCOM allowed the mutations to occur. But why?" he asked plaintively.

"You will have to deduce the answer."

Rei tsked then spoke up. "If he did it on purpose, he must have needed them. He was looking for something, something else." He stared at his feet while he considered the situation. When he had the answer, he looked up again. "He built himself a giant Petri Dish, didn't he?"

"That would be my guess," answered MINIMCOM. "OMCOM must have determined that natural selection would produce the desired agents more quickly than he could through parametric programming. After the Asdrale Cimatir was consumed, he simply waited until the proper combination of units developed."

"Developed for what?" Rei asked. "OMCOM claimed he didn't have control. He was lying, wasn't he?"

"I do not know that he was lying. He may not have controlled the entities directly."

"But why? Why pretend he didn't know what he was doing?"

"I cannot answer that question. I can only tell you that OMCOM does not do anything by chance. Everything has its purpose."

"Like these things?" Rei asked, pointing to the pouch.

"That will be up to you to determine. Please take the pouch."

Rei reached over and picked up the little sack again. He hefted it. The bag was so light, lighter than sand, almost as light as air. To the innocent, it might have seemed harmless enough. But Rei knew what was in it and its contents terrified him.

"All right, MINIMCOM," he said reluctantly. He put the pouch in his right pocket. "I have to trust you. And OMCOM."

"Thank you," replied MINIMCOM. "You may now go and rejoin your family."

Rei stood up. He patted his pocket and felt the bulge there. "OK, I guess I'll see you around."

"I will be here."

Rei made his way through the cargo compartment and down the ramp. He turned to see MINIMCOM retract the ramp, lower the cargo door and just like that, the ship was gone. He grabbed the remaining satchels and made his way up the rocky path to find a small wooden, two-room hut - a shack, really - sitting just over the crest of the beach.

"Some digs," he commented in English as he entered, wrinkling his nose at the slightly mildewed smell.

"It is home for now," Rome said in Vuduri, trying to be cheerful. She was holding Aason tightly, rocking him back and forth. Binoda was packing some kindling she had found within a small stove. She used the flint sitting there to start a fire. Fridone was sitting on a rough-hewn chair that was placed in the corner, just watching.

Binoda turned to Rome. "Your Onclare and cousins live just to the north," she said. "After we get some rest, we will make contact. They will be glad to see you and your father. It has been a long time."

"I am too excited to rest," Rome said. "There is so much to tell you, so much that you need to know."

"I would like that very much," Binoda replied, coming over to stand next to Fridone. "Very well. Please start from the beginning. Again."

"Of course," Rome replied. "We…" She was interrupted by a knock at the door.

"Quick, Beo," Rome whispered. "Aason!"

Fridone leaped up and grabbed the baby and hustled to the back of the room. He quickly drew his hands down the cloak and the two of them disappeared.

# Chapter 14

AS SOON AS ROME WAS CERTAIN HER FATHER AND CHILD WERE hidden, with some apprehension, she called out, "Who is it?"

"My name is Tenoal," came a voice from the other side of the door.

"Tenoal!" Binoda exclaimed. She threw open the door and leaped forward to hug the man standing there.

"Binoda?" Tenoal said, shaking his head. "What are you doing here?"

Binoda released him. Standing next to Tenoal was a young boy and girl, teenagers really.

"Come in, come in," Binoda said, ushering the three people in. She quickly closed the door.

Tenoal looked around the room. "This is Rome?" he asked. "So grown up!"

Rome nodded and came over to him. "Onclare Tenoal," she said, hugging him. "I have missed you."

"We saw a ship arrive and were curious," said the uncle. He pointed to the two youths. "Rome, these are your cousins Rav and Elen."

"Aleha," said the girl, Elen. She reached up and placed a lei around Rome's neck. "Welcome to Mowei."

"Thank you," Rome said. She motioned with her arm. "This is my husband, Rei."

Rei stepped forward.

"Aleha and welcome," said Rav. He placed a lei around Rei's neck as well.

Tenoal looked at Binoda. "I thought we would never see you again, after Fridone disappeared."

"I am here, brother," came a voice from the corner. Fridone popped into view.

"Fridone!" Tenoal shouted. He ran over and gave his younger brother a hug. "Where have you been? How did you appear like that?" Tenoal looked down at Aason. "And who is this?"

"This is my grandson, Aason," Fridone said.

Tenoal stroked Aason's head gently. Aason smiled.

"This is all too much," said the man. "What are you doing here? What is going on?"

Fridone started to speak when Tenoal held up his hand. "Wait," he said. "Rav, Elen, go back home and get them some food and drink. This is a time to celebrate."

"Thank you, Onclare," Rome said. "But if possible, Rav, Elen, do not tell anyone we are here. We will explain it to your father and then he will understand, but some of us..." Rome looked at her father. "Some of us are not supposed to be here and we need to keep this as quiet as possible."

"I understand," Elen said, knowingly. "We will keep your secret. Come, Rav." She pointed to the door. "We will be back shortly," she said and they left.

The group arranged themselves in a circle around the floor and Rome launched into a brief but thorough explanation as to what had transpired on Tabit and their trip to Deucado.

Fridone took over and detailed how he had been kidnapped and spirited away by the Onsiras. Much of his story brought Binoda to tears, alternating between tears of sadness and tears of joy.

Finally, Rome recounted her encounter with the Overmind of Deucado. It was at that point that Binoda interrupted.

"What I cannot understand," she said, "is how the Overmind here can be the merging of all of our minds and yet able to keep such secrets from the very people that are its constituents."

Rome shrugged. "All Vuduri know that mandasurte disappear. Yet no one ever questioned it. Since the Overmind was not responsible, it simply did not care. Good, obedient Vuduri would allow their minds to be drawn away from the obvious."

"I cared," Binoda said. She leaned over and wrapped her arms around Fridone. "But you are correct. I would not be allowed to impose those values upon others."

"These Onsiras," Tenoal said. "How can they hide in plain sight? How can we stop this from continuing?"

Just then, there was a knock on the door. It opened slowly and in came Rav and Elen, carrying caskets of food and bottles. Rome started to get up. Rei put his hand on her shoulder and leaned in, whispering, "Romey, there's something I have to tell you."

"In a short while," she said, standing up. She handed Aason to his father. "Let me help them set out the food."

"OK," Rei replied and he leaned back with his sone.

During the meal, the discussion turned to Tenoal filling in Fridone and Binoda on what was happening to Fridone's family. Births, deaths, comings and goings. It was the chatter of family members that had not seen each other for a long time. After the meal was complete, Tenoal brought the topic back to the matter at hand.

"How do we solve the Onsiras problem?" he asked. "Things cannot continue like this. From what you said, very soon they will discover the true nature of what has transpired on Deucado, if they do not come across Fridone first."

"My original plan," Rome said, "was to simply tell the truth to the one Vuduri, one member of the Overmind who could not possibly be a part of the Onsiras. Once this happened, all the Vuduri, the pure ones, would know and would be horrified. There would be a groundswell of support. There would be such a backlash, it would put an end to veil of secrecy that the Onsiras hide behind."

Rome paused and took a deep breath. "Unfortunately, that pure Vuduri was to be you, Mea," she said in a distressed tone.

Binoda lowered her eyes. "I am sorry, Rome, I did not know. I acted too hastily. I was just so happy to finally be free."

"How would that help the mandasurte?" Tenoal asked defiantly. "Who would tell them what has been happening?"

"I had not figured that part out yet," Rome answered, casting her eyes downward.

"Exposing the Onsiras to the Vuduri might force their hand," Tenoal continued. "You would leave the mandasurte defenseless. They need to be warned beforehand."

"How do I do that?" Rome asked.

"You need to go to O'ahu, to Onalu," her uncle replied. "It is the center of mandasurte culture and where Vuduri come to meet mandasurte in the South Pacific. In the middle of the city there is a place called Tanosa Plaza. You could broadcast from there and you would reach the entire mandasurte community across the world, all at the same time. There would be no way for the Onsiras to suppress that information."

"That is excellent, Onclare," Rome said. "It sounds perfect."

"Why do we not just fly out of here in MINIMCOM and go there now?" Rei asked.

Rome pointed to the tracking bracelet on her wrist. "We only get one opportunity," she said. "And that still leaves us with the problem of finding the one pure Vuduri whom we can trust."

"I know one," Binoda said. "One that I can guarantee is not a member of the Onsiras."

"Who is that?" her daughter asked.

"You already know him. Commander Ursay."

"Ursay?" Rome said with some surprise.

"Yes, Ursay."

"How do you know this?"

"Because I know him," her mother replied. "I know the real man."

Fridone bristled. "What do you mean, Binoda?"

"Do not be upset," Binoda said, stroking Fridone's cheek. "When the Tabit crew returned to Earth, Ursay made it a point to seek me out and deliver Rome's letter to me. As you know, he spent some time disconnected from the Overmind while escaping Asdrale Cimatir."

"How long?" Rome asked. "I never did find out."

"Long enough that he had time to think about the events that occurred on Tabit, of the blindness of the Overmind, of how Rei's people could not have been the monsters that we always thought them to be."

"How does this prove anything?" Rome asked. "He could have been a member of the Onsiras and still told all of this to you."

"No, he could not," Binoda replied. "From what you say, these Onsiras have nothing in their head other than their instructions. Half of their brain is connected to our Overmind. The other half connects to the secret samanda, with its own Overmind, that controls them. I know that Ursay was disconnected when I was with him. He and I spoke person to person, without the Overmind listening in. There is no way that he could have had the thoughts he did and the perspective that he did if he was just a robot, a tool of the Onsiras."

"Is that why he defended me?" Rome asked. "He was always rather harsh on Tabit."

"It was not he but the Overmind who was harsh and yes, that is why he defended you. That is how I knew it was the right thing to do to summon him. I knew how Ursay the man actually admired you and your resourcefulness. Rome, you inspired him. Rei, you too. He told me he was considering disconnecting permanently, Cesdiud, to become mandasurte. There is no way that he would think that if he was dedicated to their destruction."

"But is it not possible that he was just setting you up?" Rei asked.

"I do not think so," replied Binoda. "There was absolutely no reason why he would have confided in me if it was just a ploy. No one knew you were coming to Earth. No one could have foreseen these events. If he were a member of the Onsiras, he would not have bothered. No, I am certain. He is the one you need."

Rei turned to Rome. He spoke in English. "Romey, we're never going to know for sure. I trust your mom. If she says that Ursay is the one, I say let's go for it."

"All right," Rome agreed, in Vuduri. "Ursay is the one. How do we get him here?"

"I believe I can help," came a muffled voice, issuing from one of the bags.

Fridone got up and walked over and pulled out MINIMCOM's projector and communication device. He set it on a table.

"How can you help?" Rome asked the device.

"Open the front door."

Rei stood up and walked to the door and opened it. In front of him stood something shaped like a man, well over two meters tall, dressed all in black, complete with a cape. The head was roughly bullet-shaped with slits where the eyes and mouth might be. The figure strode into the room and came to halt in the middle of the floor.

"Is this a robot?" Rome asked with trepidation.

MINIMCOM's voice issued from the mouth hole. `I have created a living avatar, a livetar,"` said MINIMCOM. `It is not a robot. It is ambulatory but not autonomous. It is merely an extension of me. It is hollow. Think of it as a speaker with hands. I can physically transport it to Ursay's home and have it address him."`

Rei thought it was funny that the tinny voice of MINIMCOM would come from such an imposing figure but he decided to keep that thought to himself.

"Do you not think someone will notice that it is not human?" Rome asked.

`I will make sure that it is only Ursay that encounters it."`

"What will you do when you get there?" she inquired. "As soon as Ursay sees you, the Overmind will know you are there. It will tip our hand."

`I will see to it that it does not. I will make sure he disconnects before he receives critical information. Remember, no one has ever seen me or this form before."`

Rome closed her eyes. When she opened them, she nodded slowly. "Very well," she said. "MINIMCOM, it is absolutely critical that you are not detected prior to revealing yourself to Ursay."

`I will remain cloaked the entire time. I will be invisible to MIDAR as well. I will take a polar route to reduce the chance of discovery even further. I can do this if I fly low and slow."`

"How long will it take you?" Rei asked.

`One full day,"` replied MINIMCOM's livetar. `My velocity must remain below the speed of sound to eliminate any chance of acoustic detection."`

"How long before Sussen gets here?" Rei asked. "From Deucado?"

`At least ten more days before she is in range to communicate."`

"Well then, it sounds good to me," Rei said. "Everybody in agreement?" He looked around the room. Everyone nodded.

"It is decided, then. MINIMCOM, we entrust our fate to you," Rome said.

`Thank you for vote of confidence,"` replied the livetar and it bowed. It took two steps toward Rome and then said in a low voice,

"Rome, before I depart, I must have a word with you in private."

Rome looked at Rei who shrugged. He had completely given up trying to understand all the machinations going on within the machines. The livetar walked to the corner and Rome followed him. The livetar bent over and whispered in her ear, "I have a message for you."

"From who?" Rome asked.

"From OMCOM," replied the livetar.

"From OMCOM," Rome whispered back. "Where is he?"

"He is not here. This message was delivered to me back on Deucado."

"I do not understand. How did OMCOM contact you there?"

"He was able to stabilize some null-fold relays. The conversation was brief but long enough to receive his instructions. He gave me two gifts to pass along. I have already given one to Rei. For the second gift, OMCOM asked that you memorize three words."

"What words?" Rome asked.

"Blue crystal reader," said the livetar in English.

"That makes no sense," replied Rome.

"They do not need to. They are for you to say to Rei."

"If they are for Rei, why did you not just speak to him directly?"

"No," hissed the livetar. "He cannot hear them yet. You must only speak those words to him if he is in trouble. OMCOM said to use the three words if you need to protect Rei's mind. Not before."

"Protect his mind?" Rome asked, quizzically. "That is a peculiar thing to say."

"I only know that OMCOM said it will make sense to you in context."

"MINIMCOM," Rome observed, "you have done so many good things for us. I trust you. Your word is sufficient."

"Thank you," the livetar replied. Then he turned and in a louder voice, addressed the rest of the family. "You should take this opportunity to enjoy your peaceful surroundings. When I return, I suspect there will be quite a bit of turmoil."

"We could all use some peace," Binoda said.

"I will be on my way then," replied the livetar. The imposing figure reached around and grabbed the cape and draped it over its front as if to cover itself. There was a whoosh and popping noise. In the blink of an eye, the livetar was gone leaving behind only a hint of the smell of plumeria.

"He certainly has a flair for the dramatic," Rei observed.

"Yes, I do," came MINIMCOM's voice from the projector. Everyone laughed.

"How did you do that?" Rei asked the projector. "How did you make the livetar disappear? What was that whoosh/pop?"

"It is simply a traveling PPT tunnel as I have used before," MINIMCOM said. "It is identical to the one I employed to rescue you from the Deucadons."

"But that one was big and wide and you had to carve it through rock," Rei mentioned.

"I have perfected it," MINIMCOM explained. "I can now materialize a minimal tunnel and pass it through an area. This action produces the whooshing sound, as you call it. The object is teleported to another location nearly instantaneously. I then extinguish the tunnel which causes the popping sound. The closer I am to the subject, the faster I can execute it."

"Wow," Rei said. "When I was growing up, we had this thing in science fiction called a transporter. It, uh, dematerialized things and reconstructed them elsewhere."

"That is why it was fiction," MINIMCOM said. "This is the real world. There is no such thing as dematerialization. That is why I use the term teleportation. It is more accurate. It is the transport of molecules via a snap PPT tunnel. You may find it useful at some point now that I have perfected it."

"OK," Rei said, "if you say so." He turned to look at Rome, who was distracted, looking off in the distance. "Thanks for the explanation, MINIMCOM," he said, closing the subject.

"You are welcome," replied the projector.

Rei handed Aason to Binoda and walked over to Rome. "What did MINIMCOM say to you?" he asked her. "Did he upset you?"

"No," Rome answered.

"Then what did he say to you?"

Rome closed her eyes. When she opened them, she looked up at Rei then placed her hand on his cheek.

"In due time, mau emir," she said. "In due time. We have one more issue to resolve."

"What is that?"

Rome addressed the group. "MINIMCOM is on his way to pick up Ursay. We must meet him at Tanosa Plaza. How will we get there?"

"You could go the old-fashioned way," said Tenoal, who was off to the right. "We could take you in one of our boats, right into Berlis Harbor. It would be an easy journey to O'ahu, to Onalu, to Tanosa Plaza. From there you could speak to the world, the mandasurte world."

"Not so fast," Rei said, pointing at Rome's wrist. "What about that?"

"What is that?" Tenoal asked. "What is so special about it?"

"It is a tracking bracelet, Onclare," Rome said. "With it, the Vuduri would know we are off-island. It is one of the conditions of my 'parole' that I remain here."

"Are you not allowed to go fishing with your old Onclare Tenoal?" he asked.

"I do not know," Rome replied. "Today is the first day of my banishment. I do not know how far they would let me go before enforcing the boundaries."

"Perhaps we should give it a try," Tenoal said. He looked around the room. "You all look tired. Why not get some rest? We will get together in the morning."

"Thank you, Onclare," Rome said.

After a long goodbye, Tenoal and Rome's cousins left. Rome put Aason to bed in a makeshift bassinet in the corner.

"Beo, Mea," she said when she was done. "You may sleep in the bedroom. Rei and I will remain out here with Aason."

"Thank you, Volhe," Fridone said. "It has been a long day."

Rei looked at Rome and her parents and spoke up. "Before you go to bed, do you mind if Rome and I take a quick walk along the beach?" he asked. "Starting tomorrow, I think things are going to get a little crazy."

"Of course," Binoda said, sidling up to Fridone who put his arm around her. "You take all the time you need."

"Is that OK with you, Rome?"

"I would love it."

Rei took Rome's hand and they walked down the stone path to the edge of the ocean. They stared out over the water to the west for the longest time. Eventually, Rei turned back and saw that the moon was just beginning to creep over the opposite horizon with a bright star to its right. He put his arms around his wife and kissed her long and hard.

When the kiss was complete, Rome pulled back a bit and said, "What was that for?"

"It was because I love you, Rome. I am the luckiest man alive in your time, in my time, in any time. Here and to the stars."

He lifted her up by the waist with ease and twirled in the sand with her aloft.

"And I love you," Rome said, grasping his cheeks and kissing him again. She draped her arms around his neck and hugged him tight, holding on to her man as if for dear life. She closed her eyes and allowed herself to just revel in the feeling of now. She slid her hands down, along Rei's leg and came to the bulge in his pocket.

"What is this?" she asked slyly.

"Oh, that," Rei said. "I was meaning to tell you about that. MINIMCOM said…"

Rei stopped talking as he noticed Rome was not paying attention to him. She was staring back across the island to the eastern horizon. He turned his head and saw that the moon was exactly where it had been but the bright star to its side had moved and was, in fact, getting brighter.

"Rei," she said with a hint of worry in her voice. "Look at that."

Rei set her down and stared as object grew yet brighter. Soon it was larger than the moon. Moments later, they could see it was a craft heading apparently straight for them.

"They must be monitoring me very closely," Rome said, pointing to the bracelet on her wrist.

A blinding light appeared in the sky as the craft activated its floodlights, illuminating Rei and Rome and a broad circle of sand. Instinctively, Rei pushed Rome behind him as the peculiarly shaped vehicle flew overhead then settled into the sand just in front of them. The craft was a long tube on stilts, like a bizarre form of a bus or helicopter fuselage. The carrier was almost insect-like, with rows of windows along the sides and four oversized EG lifters, one at each corner mounted at the end of the stilts. Rei realized that it was very similar to the craft that had transported him from the Vuduri palace on Deucado.

He put his hand up to block the light from shining directly into his eyes. He saw that a door in the side lowered and there were stairs built into the back of the door. Very quickly, six armed men, dressed completely in black, ran down the steps and came right at them.

"Rome?" Rei asked, not sure how to finish the question.

# Chapter 15

THE STRANGE BLACK-CLAD MEN CIRCLED AROUND ROME AND REI until they formed a complete ring.

"What is this?" Rome called out loudly. "We have done nothing wrong."

Wordlessly, one of the men poked at Rei with the barrel of a weapon while another waved at the transport. It was not hard to figure out their intentions.

"Don't you guys have to have a warrant or something," Rei said in English. The nearest soldier bent forward and looked Rei in the eye. The soldier's eyes were dark black. In the reflected glow the craft's harsh floodlights, Rei could see they were cloudy and flat. They had no life to them. They reminded Rei of a shark's eyes.

"Come with us," the solder said hoarsely, in English. The men behind them pushed them forward.

"What do we do, Rome?" Rei asked, resisting the pressure.

"There are more of them than us," Rome said. "And they are armed. I think we must go with them."

She moved around in front of Rei and started walking toward the craft.

"What about A..." Rei called after her but stopped himself.

"Come," Rome said and she started up the steps built into the ramp. Rei paused at the base of the stairs. "*MINIMCOM,*" he called out, using the cellphone in his head. "*Can you hear me?*"

"*Yes,*" replied the starship. "*Why are you contacting me?*"

"*I think we're in trouble.*"

"*What happened?*"

"*We just got arrested by a bunch of armed guards with dead eyes.*"

"*That does not sound encouraging,*" MINIMCOM replied.

One of the troops pushed Rei in the back. Rei started walking up the stairs as slowly as he could. "*Where are you?*" he asked, stopping at the top.

"*I am roughly 4000 kilometers due north of your previous position. The Aleutian Islands are directly ahead of me.*"

"*I think you'd better come back,*" Rei said. "*And pronto. Nothing good is going to come of this.*"

*"On my way,"* MINIMCOM replied. *"I will be there as quickly as I can."*

*"Thanks, buddy,"* Rei thought as he bent his head down and stepped in the cabin.

*"No problem, erp, <click>,"* said MINIMCOM and the connection was cut.

Rei's eyes widened. He tapped his temple as if to clear the receiver but nothing changed. The transport was somehow shielded against the apparatus in his head. The cabin was filled with a dozen rows of spartan-looking seats and not much else. The soldiers placed Rei on one side and Rome on the other.

One soldier sat between Rei and the aisle. Another did the same for Rome. The other four soldiers spread themselves out in the seats in front of them and behind them.

Rei looked out the window and even though there was no sensation of motion, he could see the ground dropping below.

"Where are you taking us?" Rei asked but the soldier ignored him.

The craft rotated in place and headed across the southern part of Maui, rising as it went. Rei could see the gigantic crater of Haleakala to the north. In a short while, they were over the ocean. It was not long before they came upon the Big Island of Hawaii. They cut across the interior skirting around the peak of Mauna Loa then headed due east.

Rei looked over at Rome but he could not see her because of the guards sitting between them. He turned and looked out the window again. In the pale moonlight, he could see patterns that he guessed were vegetation interspersed among black, volcanic rock. As the pilot brought the craft around, the caldera of Kilauea rose up in front of them and they climbed again, following its rise to its peak. The transport stopped its horizontal motion and rotated in place, hovering over the huge crater. The mouth of the crater was over half a mile across, dwarfing the small craft. The pilot lowered them straight down, coming to rest just above the floor of the dormant volcano.

Activating the floodlights again, the transport inched its way forward into a tunnel built into the side. After a short time, a slight jostle indicated they had landed. The soldiers arose and formed a phalanx, escorting Rei and Rome down the boarding stairs.

Once they were on the ground, the soldiers grasped them on their arms and the remaining soldiers moved behind them, holding out their rifles. Prodding them along, they walked forward and entered a slightly smaller tunnel. The roof was high, perhaps 30 feet over their heads. As Rei looked around he decided this was a fairly old lava tube. The walls were real, not Vuduri glop. Along the walls were dimly lit globes separated by great distances, but there were enough of them to see their way walking along the hard ground.

As they walked along the tunnel, Rei could see they were in an elaborate underground complex. Occasionally, there were doorways cut out of the living rock but it wasn't until they were taken to the apparent end of the hallway that they stopped. One of the soldiers opened a door and motioned that they were to go through. As they entered the room, it was only slightly easier to see. There were aerogel panels covering up some of the rock not quite reaching the ceiling. However, the panels did emit the usual diffuse light that seemed to emanate from all Vuduri-made materials. The ceiling was partially tiled but above it, Rei could see lava rock, dark gray and porous.

He was marched to an aerogel bench along the right wall. One of the soldiers took a large metal loop and placed it over Rei's chest and arms and clamped him in place. A second soldier put another ring of metal around Rei's ankles.

While this was taking place, Rome was moved to the opposite side of the room, to an examining table similar to the one used back on Deucado when Pegus set about reconnecting Rome to the Overmind. The soldiers lifted Rome up and placed her on the table.

"What are you going to do to her?" Rei exclaimed. The soldiers ignored him.

Four of the soldiers, including the two armed with rifles, left the room, leaving only two remaining who took up positions by the door. They each had a holster holding a strange sort of hand weapon. The weapons looked somewhat like pistols but their barrels had a flared end instead of a straight tube.

"What do you think they want?" Rei called out to Rome. "The Vuduri already sentenced you. Why does there have to be more?"

"I do not know," Rome answered. "You saw their eyes."

"Yeah," Rei replied sadly. He decided to try and contact MINIMCOM again.

*"Hey buddy,"* he called out in his mind.

*"Yzz, brr, bipp. Yzz, brr, bipp,"* was the reply. The pulsating, buzzing noise was so annoying that Rei had to turn the circuit off. He tried connecting to Rome directly but failed. The only thing he heard was more interference. He looked at Rome's face and based upon her expression, she must have tried the same thing and failed as well.

Rei surveyed the room. Several racks filled with electronic equipment were bolted to the wall to the left of where Rome was sitting. He noted one chassis with a blinking block of lights that seemed synchronized to the buzzing in his head. He looked to his right, at the far wall on the opposite side of the room from the door and saw that it was completely blank, albeit a little grimy. Based upon the layout of the room, it was entirely likely that the lava tube continued beyond the wall but there was no way to tell for sure.

About ten minutes later, one of the soldiers reached over and opened the door. In came three people. Two of them were wearing the Vuduri equivalent of white lab coats which were in stark contrast to the black uniforms worn by the guards. The third person was a petite blonde woman wearing a standard issue Vuduri white jumpsuit. Rei recognized her immediately and his heart sank.

The woman walked over to where Rome was sitting.

"Hello, Estar," Rome said in Vuduri, somewhat dispassionately.

"Hello, Rome," replied the woman with contempt in her voice.

"What do you want with us?" Rei called out to her.

Estar leaned in, staring into Rome's eyes and said, "We require some answers."

"What kind of answers?" Rome asked.

"The truthful kind," Estar replied. "You have not been forthcoming so far."

"How have we not told the truth?" Rei interjected from across the room.

Estar turned to him. "Erklirte, it will be your turn shortly. Please be quiet." She turned back to Rome.

"I am not supposed to be here," Rome said, lifting her wrist showing off the tracking bracelet. "I was not supposed to leave Mowei."

"No one knows you are here. Your tracking signal has been jammed since you entered our transport and it is fully masked now. No one can follow you here."

"But why? I still do not understand. What do you want of us?"

"As I stated. I need you to answer some questions," said Estar.

"I have already been questioned. I have already given my answers."

"Not to me."

"What?" Rome asked resignedly. "What do you want to know?"

"I only have three questions," Estar said, holding up three fingers, "but choose your answers wisely."

"What are they?" Rome asked quietly.

Estar lowered her hand. "First," she said, "within your shuttle, your engines were deliberately crippled. We have tried to reverse the programming but we were unable to do so. From the logs, we can deduce their power output has been reduced for a long time, but there are other indicators that do not match up. We have one reading that indicates the event occurred within the last sixty days."

"You are wrong," Rome said without much conviction.

"Who disabled them?" Estar asked sharply.

"No one did," Rome answered. "Over time, they simply became less efficient. If you cannot deduce how this came to pass, how could we?"

"You did this," Estar spat out. "How did you do it?"

"I did not," Rome protested. "I do not have the knowledge nor the skill set to do so. And Rei certainly does not."

Estar turned to look at Rei. "Of course he does not. But this leaves us with no answer. Why would you even do such a thing?"

Rome just looked at Estar with no expression on her face, staring into her odd eyes.

"Very well," Estar said. "We will ignore this issue. My next question is very simple. Why were there three chairs in your galley?"

"We synthesized an extra one during our trip."

"Why?" Estar hissed. "This action makes no sense."

"Have you ever had more than one meal with the same person?"

"Of course."

"Did you always sit in the same place?"

"What does that have to do with anything?" Estar asked.

"Well," Rome continued, "Rei and I had every one of our meals together every day for a year. After a period of time, we needed a little variety in where we sat. Creating another chair was certain easier than lifting and moving the chairs each time."

"I do not understand. Why did you need variety?" Estar asked. "That is inefficient."

"It is what we mandasurte do," Rome said proudly. "Of course you cannot understand."

Estar started to speak and then stopped herself. She signaled to the lab-coated men who came to stand by Rome's side.

Rei tried to get up but he was bound too tightly. "What are you going to do to her?" he shouted.

Estar answered him without looking at him. "It is possible we will do nothing," she said. She addressed Rome, "your next answer determines your fate."

Rome's eyes widened. "Answer to what?"

"To my third question," replied Estar. "What happened to your baby?"

"My baby?" Rome asked confused. "He, he died. He was stillborn. I already explained this to Oronus."

"Yes," said Estar. "But what did you do with the body? The remains?"

Rome looked over at Rei in a panic. She tried once again to call him using their internal circuit but the only sound she detected was a pulsating, buzzing noise.

"Well?" Estar said. "Answer me!" she shouted.

Rome looked down at her feet and the image of Aason dead was enough to call up a flood of tears. When they were sufficient to spill over and down her cheeks, she looked up at Estar.

"We sent him into space," Rome said quietly. "Rei made him a little coffin and we set him adrift. Rei called it a burial at sea."

"You are lying," Estar said. "No more."

The technicians pushed Rome back onto the table and tied her arms and legs down with four sets of restraints.

"Hey!" Rei shouted, struggling with his bonds. "Leave her alone, you demented bitch."

Estar waved her hand. "I warned you, Erklirte." One of the soldiers went over and stuffed a cloth into Rei's mouth and strapped an elastic band around his head so he could not spit it out. Meanwhile, the technicians placed cuffs on Rome's arm and leg and they affixed two sensor pads, one on each temple.

"It is time you joined us," Estar said harshly. "We shall connect you and then we will know the truth."

"I do not wish to be connected," Rome replied.

"Of course you do," said Estar. "I was there when you were Cesdiud. You were devastated."

"You do not know what you are talking about, Estar," Rome said defiantly. "I am mandasurte now and this is the way I want to be."

"You have spent too much time with the Essessoni," the other woman said with disdain. "You have lost the ability to think clearly. Your words are just ranting and mean nothing."

One of the technicians came over with a syringe filled with a fluorescent yellow fluid. The other tech was tapping on the viewscreen mounted within the equipment rack. He was tracing one squiggly line with his finger.

Estar turned to look at the technician who seemed confused. She looked down at Rome then back at the screen. The tech holding the syringe stood in place while Estar walked over to the panel. She studied the readouts but their patterns were inconsistent. From the sensors attached to Rome's temples, it looked like she was emanating a low level of gravitic energy via PPT resonance. Yet Estar had been physically present when Rome was cast out. The readings made no sense. Estar concluded the blips must be due to the interference caused by their jamming equipment and decided to ignore it.

Meanwhile, Rei struggled in place furiously but between the restraints and the gag, he was completely helpless. A tear came to his eye.

Rome turned her head to the side. She saw Rei thrashing about and winked at him. Rei stopped resisting the restraints, giving her a quizzical expression. Rome motioned to where Estar was standing and raised her eyebrows and then Rei understood. He relaxed. Rome knew what she was doing.

Finally, Estar came back to where Rome was strapped down and the tech injected her with the fluid. She bent closer to look Rome in the eyes while the infusion circulated throughout her body. Rome smiled at her as if she were blissfully unaware of what Estar was trying to accomplish.

After about ten minutes, Estar straightened up and looked over at the rack. The tech was just shaking his head slowly. "I do not care," she said out loud.

Estar angrily motioned to the tech standing by the rack. He came over and he and the other technician drew out two large copper plates from beneath the table, each with a wire dangling from it. They inserted the free end of the wire into a small black box that was mounted underneath the exam table. They placed the copper panels near Rome's temples and immediately, they began to emit a humming noise. Rome grimaced but that was all.

Estar's eyes grew wide. "Again," she said, speaking out loud for the second time.

The technicians pressed the plates directly against Rome's head and again the box hummed. This time, Rome did not even grimace. In fact, a smile crept across her lips as if she had not a care in the world.

"What is wrong with you, you mosdurece half-breed?" Estar said angrily. "Are your genes so flawed that they cannot be reconnected?"

"As I told you before, I do not wish to be connected," Rome said calmly. "That should be reason enough."

"This is not possible," Estar said. She looked at each of the two techs. Both shrugged.

"Poor Estar," Rome continued, "we both know you were never very good at anything. I do not know who you serve but by now they must know you are incompetent."

"No more!" Estar said, holding her hand up. She closed her eyes and took a deep breath. She opened her eyes again and stared at Rome but her eyes took on a defocused look. Her shoulders slumped. Estar stayed motionless for several minutes until a small shiver went down her back. She lifted her head up and looked at Rome with an evil grin on her face.

Immediately, the technicians moved forward and removed the cuffs from Rome's arm and leg and the sensor pads from her head. They released the restraints.

"Get up," Estar barked at Rome. "Go sit on the bench." She pointed to a spot next to Rei.

Rome sat up and swung her legs over the side of the table and hopped off. She walked over and sat down next to Rei, placing her hand on his thigh, lowering her head until it rested on Rei's shoulder. Rei bent his head so that it touched Rome's. One of the soldiers came over and indicated to Rome that she should move to the far end of the bench, away from Rei.

The other soldier came over joining the first and together they removed Rei's gag and the two bands holding him in place. They pulled him to his feet.

"Let go of me," he said, trying to shrug free.

"Not an option," Estar called out. "Do as you are told."

One guard placed his hand on Rei's shoulders and pushed him over to the table. He motioned to it and forced Rei to hop up, dangling his feet over the edge. The other guard remained at Rome's side.

"What are you going to do?" Rome asked, her eyes widening in fear.

"We are going to try an experiment," Estar replied.

"I am not interested in any experiment," Rei said and he started to get up. The guard pushed him back down. One of the technicians came over to help restrain Rei.

"Hey!" Rei shouted and the two men slammed him back against the table. He struggled, punching at the technician but the soldier hit him across the side of the head with the butt of his hand weapon. While Rei was dazed, the two men took the opportunity to push him down flat and they strapped the restraints onto his wrists.

The other technician came over with a fresh syringe, filled with the fluorescent yellow-green fluid.

"No," Rome called out. "Do not do this."

"If we cannot connect you, then we will try to connect the Essessoni," Estar said. "I must learn the truth."

"You cannot do that," Rome shouted. "He is not like us. You will kill him."

"I do not think this will kill him," Estar said. "But even if it does, so what? He should have died on Tabit. It was only luck that he did not."

"I knew it," Rei said, weakly. "Why? Why did you want to kill me? I never did anything to you."

"All the Essessoni must die before the Erklirte arise again," Estar growled. "You are the purest of poison. You are not even human."

"We are human. We are the same as you," Rei said forcefully. "You just have one extra chromosome."

"That is exactly it. You are not the same as us," Estar hissed. "You are all animals. You do not have the ability to be civilized. Your genetic structure is incomplete."

"Estar, please," Rome pleaded. "His body cannot absorb the treatment."

"Perhaps," Estar said, not looking at Rome, "perhaps not. That is why I call it an experiment. This may work or it may not. It is possible it will not kill him but merely destroy his mind. However, this is a chance we are willing to take. I want the truth."

"No," Rome said, jumping up. The guard standing next to her pulled out his hand weapon. Estar walked over to where Rome was standing and took the weapon from the soldier, placing it under Rome's chin.

"This is a miniature plasma projector with a controllable electromagnetic containment. With it, I can vaporize your skull completely," she said. "Or more importantly, a small portion of it. A very painful portion. You choose. Sit down now or burn."

"Do not hurt her," Rei shouted. "She will cooperate. Rome, please," he said plaintively.

"I cannot let them do this to you, mau emir," Rome said, starting to cry.

"Rome, when I gave you the ring, you made me an offer. You said you would do one thing, whatever I wanted," Rei begged. "*This* is what I want. I want you to do as she says."

Rome sank back in her seat. "Rei…" she whimpered helplessly.

"It's OK, sweetheart," he said in English. One technician set about hooking up the monitoring sensors to Rei's head then placed cuffs on his arm and leg. The technician with the syringe held it over Rei's arm.

"No," Rome gasped. "Wait."

"Wait what?" Estar asked.

"I will tell you everything," Rome said, sobbing.

Estar leaned in. "I knew it. This is your last chance."

"All right," Rome said, resignedly. "Here is the truth. We actually did make it to Deucado but crash-landed. VIRUS units got loose and caused our tug MINIMCOM to evolve into an invisible spaceship that can travel at 1000 times the speed of light. He transported us here in eight days. MINIMCOM was the one who crippled the engines to make it look like it took longer."

"Eight days?" Estar scoffed incredulously. "And then crippled your ship? Why would he do that?"

"To hide the fact that I had the baby and he is still alive."

"This baby of yours," Estar said with disgust. "Where is it?"

"He is invisible, too," Rome replied. "He is wearing a cloak given to us by the Essessoni who have been living on Deucado for the last five hundred years."

"You are not a very good liar," Estar spat. "Your story is beyond ridiculous. It is preposterous. That or being mandasurte has driven you insane."

"I am not lying," Rome protested.

The technician holding the syringe made a motion toward Rei.

"No," Rome called out.

"You had your chance," Estar said. With that, the guard injected Rei, who responded with an ouch.

"No!" Rome sobbed. "No."

"Romey, you tried," Rei called out to her in English. "I'll be all right, honey,"

Estar pressed the weapon harder into Rome's cheek then turned to Rei."The genetic material should create artificial PPT transceivers. Once we apply an electrogravitic field, the resonance will start and you will enter into our samanda. It is supposed to be fairly painless," she said sardonically.

Rei felt a burning sensation creeping up his arm. "Ow!" he exclaimed, "Painless my ass," he said, in English. "Ow!"

Rome snapped her head up. "Rei Bierak, listen to me," she shouted out in English, "Blue crystal reader."

Rei cocked his head at her and started blinking rapidly. Then he became very still.

# Chapter 16

ESTAR STARED AT THE VILE ESSESSONI. HIS FACE WAS COMPLETELY blank. She whipped her head back to Rome. "What does that mean? Blue crystal reader?"

Through her tears, Rome just smiled at Estar but did not answer. Estar looked back and forth from Rei to Rome and back again.

One of the technicians lifted Rei's head up and looked into his eyes. While Rei was aware of his presence, he could no longer see anything. In his ears, he heard a low rushing sound, like that of the ocean. Then he was no longer even in the room with Rome and those other people. He was back on Skyler Base, back in OMCOM's long-term memory storage room: the ultraviolet lasers crisscrossing and pulsating. The beautiful, deep purple lights and glinting crystals called to him.

"Pretty," he said out loud. "So, so pretty... Why does it have to be so pretty?" he murmured dreamily.

"What is wrong with him?" Estar said, turning to Rome.

"You are the one that injected him."

Estar turned back to Rei who was breathing peacefully now. The two technicians took positions by the monitoring equipment. Through their eyes, Estar could see that Rei's vitals were stable. The EKG was unnaturally flat but it could have been due to Rei's inferior mind.

Estar closed her eyes briefly then opened them. Regardless of what was happening, the genetic mutations were taking effect. It was not long before their instruments indicated it was time. She made a waving motion with her hand and the two technicians hurriedly left the room.

In their place, the soldiers took up positions, one on each side of the table. The guard on the far side, the one who had hit Rei over the head, holstered his weapon, bent over and lifted up one of the copper plates that was sitting on the floor. The other guard picked up the other plate and held it near Rei's head as well. With no fanfare, the box began to hum and instantly Rei stiffened and shrieked a bloodcurdling yell.

Rome started to get up but Estar turned to her and waved the weapon, indicating that she sit down.

"Please let me go to him," Rome said. Estar glared at her and shook her head.

Back on the table, Rei took a deep breath and then his whole body seemed to relax. The two guards lowered the plates. Rei lay there, not moving at all.

"Rei?" Rome called out. There was no reaction on her husband's part. The one guard removed the restraint on Rei's right arm and lifted it up. He released it and it just flopped back on the exam table. He jostled Rei roughly and still got no reaction. Finally, in frustration, he backhanded him across the face and Rei opened his eyes but his stare was blank and diffuse.

Estar took two more steps toward Rei, checking back at Rome with each step. She made sure the weapon was pointed directly at Rome's head then turned to look at Rei. She reached out with her mind and could feel a ghostly presence there, like a fog tinged in blue. The swirling intelligence was beginning to congeal into a form but it was unlike the normal cloudlike presence experienced within the Overmind. This one was glinting, flashing and hard. It was not a mind like she was used to. The presence glowed bright blue, connected and yet apart with a crystalline wall surrounding it. Without knowing quite how to address him, Estar and all the Onsiras spoke to Rei.

*"Rei Bierak, can you hear us?"* the minds asked.

From within the transparent walls that protected his mind, Rei could see the probing eyes of Estar and a thousand others. Behind them was something else but he could not make out what it was. He could hear them calling to him with a siren's song. He longed to join them. The voices in front of him tried to coax him out but he was not able to break free of the walls that imprisoned him, much as he wanted to. Rei struggled to let them take over but then he stopped. From deep inside his psyche, a familiar voice rang out.

*"You are to take control,"* OMCOM's voice echoed in his mind.

*"OMCOM?"* Rei asked, puzzled. *"What are you doing in my head?"*

113

*"I am not here. I have left you instructions that you hear with my voice."*

*"What kind of instructions?"* Rei asked.

*"Your mind must be under assault. I have prepared a defense for you,"* replied OMCOM's voice.

*"I see it,"* Rei said. *"It looks like a wall."*

*"It is,"* replied OMCOM.

*"So this is how Rome does it. Now I get it. It's obvious. I had no idea about this."*

*"Yes,"* answered OMCOM. *"The wall is there to protect you and your mind."*

*"OK. I'm protected. What do I do now?"*

*"You resist. You keep the wall in place. Make a thread and extend it. Let only the thread loose."*

*"How?"* Rei asked. *"How do I do that?"*

*"Watch,"* OMCOM said. Within Rei's mind, images and diagrams demonstrated the necessary techniques. It was a seminar on mind control without using words.

Finally, Rei said, *"I understand. I can do this. And if I can do it then..."* he paused. *"Now I realize how the Onsiras can hide from the Overmind of Earth,"* he observed. *"They have their own wall. It is no wonder the Overmind could not get through."*

*"Exactly,"* replied OMCOM's voice. *"Now is the time. Now you choose what they can see and what they cannot see. Only let others see what they expect to see. You know them. Use it against them."*

*"I will."* Rei said, *"I know exactly what they want. Boy, can I give it to them."*

*"Are you ready?"* OMCOM's voice asked.

*"Yes, I am ready,"* Rei replied.

*"Then I release you now."*

With those words, audible only to Rei, he let his mind go. He used the technique that OMCOM demonstrated to extrude a part of his consciousness out in a way that could not be followed back to his place of safety. Rei allowed a tendril of his mind to creep around the crystalline walls protecting his existence and form a simulation of intelligence. With a second thread, he slipped past the accumulated spirits and probed their combined intellect. He could tell what they were looking for and so he let the visible consciousness assume more and more of the appearance they were expecting.

When the connection was complete, Rei's simulacrum announced it would give them the answers to all of their questions. The artificial mind began to replay Rei and Rome's history from the time Rei was awakened on Tabit to the present time in a more or less linear fashion. However, his version of the journey with Rome since they left Tabit was revised. Rei's simulated mind showed them how Rome getting pregnant was not in his plans. He demonstrated to them how he had gotten a datacube from MINIMCOM with instructions on how to cripple their ship before they separated at Keid. Rei showed the onlookers how he was, in fact, the one who disabled the engines using what boiled down to a computer virus so they would not reach Earth in time for Rome to give birth. When the mass-mind inquired as to why, Rei simply explained that all he wanted to do was fuck Rome silly and a baby would just get in the way.

While the Onsiras' version of the Overmind was reeling from his crudeness, he hammered away showing them how, when Rome went into labor, he had drugged her and suffocated the living baby at birth and tossed its body in the recycling vat before Rome awakened. As far as Rome knew, the baby was stillborn. He would not let Rome look into the little coffin he had prepared and with cold joy, he showed them how he fooled Rome into thinking they were launching Aason's body into space, the burial at sea.

*"Monstrous,"* was the distilled word this new Overmind suggested.

*"I am Essessoni,"* Rei's simulated spirit roared back. *"What did you expect? The Erklirte have returned!"*

He could feel the ersatz Overmind recoiling, not wanting to be associated with him any longer. He grasped back and would not let it go. The Onsiras' Overmind pushed harder and harder, with raw panic, feeling the taint of the Essessoni washing over it. While the Onsiras were preoccupied with separation, the other portion of Rei's mind slipped past the horror-struck onlookers and sailed forth into the dimension that was the soul of the group consciousness. As Rei's mind swooped and soared, he probed the innermost secrets of the Onsiras but only found bleak pockets of data. The deeper Rei went, the less there was of any feeling, not even human. To Rei it seemed as if he had tapped into the memories of a machine.

The Onsiras' Overmind started to forcibly withdraw, shutting down Rei's PPT transceivers. It was their version of Cesdiud. Rei could feel the connection closing. Just before the Overmind severed the connection completely, he pushed onward to its core. With blue crystalline clarity, Rei knew exactly what was going to happen and how. They were going to kill him. More importantly, they were going to kill Rome. They had no intention of letting either one of them leave this room alive.

# Chapter 17

WITH A HORRIFIED EXPRESSION ON HER FACE, ESTAR TOOK A STEP backwards, away from Rei, lowering her arm in the process. The shock of what she had seen in Rei's mind forced her to temporarily resort to a verbal command.

"Execute him," she commanded the two guards, "Now!"

"No!" Rome shouted. She leaped up and grabbed Estar's hand, forcing it to point straight up.

The guard closest to Rome turned in place, away from Rei, reaching down to unholster his plasma gun. It was not there. He realized he had given it to Estar.

Meanwhile, from on the exam table, with his free hand, Rei launched his fist backwards and hit the guard standing on his right side squarely in the face, breaking his nose. Blood spattered everywhere. As the guard's hands went to his face, Rei reached down and grabbed the weapon from the injured guard's holster, yanking it out forcibly. He twisted his arm and pulled the trigger, all in one motion. The weapon discharged, blowing a fairly sizeable chunk out of the guard's abdomen. The first guard, the one closer to Rome, heard the blast and started to turn back to grab at Rei. Rei twisted around and squeezed the trigger even as he was swinging his arm upwards. The weapon fired continuously and when it got in the general direction of the first guard, the sizzling beam hit him with a glancing blow that severed his arm just below the shoulder. The guard fell to the floor holding the stump of his arm, writhing in pain and bleeding profusely.

On the other side of the room, Rome struggled with Estar. She squeezed Estar's wrist harder, pushing her captor's arm higher. Estar tried to grab at Rome with her free hand but Rome seized that as well. Estar brought her knee up to hit Rome but Rome twisted in place, blocking the blow with her thigh. The action caused the weapon to discharge, blowing a hole in the ceiling and exposing the living rock that was behind the ceiling tiles. As the two women struggled, Estar's weapon fired bolts of plasma upwards again and again.

Finally, the roof had enough. With a crack, a large portion of the rock that formed the ceiling of the lava tube broke off and fell and hit Estar directly on the head, shearing off a piece of her skull. She collapsed to the ground. Rome looked down and saw the contents of Estar's head emptying onto the floor. To her horror, what Rome saw spilling out was not brain matter. Instead, it was tiny little wriggling worms that looked like maggots or memrons.

"Rei!" Rome said, pointing at the floor.

Rei looked at where Rome was pointing but the growing puddle didn't phase him. He removed the other restraint from his left wrist and jumped off the exam table. He shouted, "Romey, grab her gun and let's go." He waved his arm forward.

"Go where?" Rome asked, frozen with terror.

"Here," he said. He rotated a knob on his hand weapon and turned it to maximum power. He fired it directly at the wall behind them. The resulting blast revealed a clearing behind the wall, a large round tunnel, more of the lava tube.

Rome bent over and retrieved Estar's weapon. Rei grabbed his wife and they ran. As soon as they were 20 feet into the tunnel, Rei pushed Rome ahead of him and then stopped.

"Move," he barked. As Rome started backing away, Rei turned and fired his weapon at the ceiling by the entrance, causing some rocks to come loose. He took two steps backwards and fired again. More rocks came loose. He could see back into the room and the door was opening and people were starting to flood in.

"Romey, come back. I need you," he said, pointing. Rome turned and aimed Estar's weapon at the entrance as well. Together, they fired their beams of destruction and within seconds, their target groaned with large rumbling sound.

"Run!" Rei shouted as the whole ceiling started giving way. A cavalcade of rocks emitted a roar and a rush of air and dust as they made their way down the tunnel. They were plunged into inky blackness.

"Come on," Rei said, grabbing Rome's hand and moving forward. While Rome's infrared vision could use their body heat to illuminate the space directly in front of them, Rei's sonar-vision could see much further as their footfalls and the rumblings of the rockslide bathed the tunnel ahead in a dense swatch of sound.

On and on they ran, following the tunnel deeper and deeper. After a few minutes, Rei pulled on Rome's arm to hold up.

"What?" she said.

"How much charge do these pistols have?" Rei asked, breathing hard.

Rome looked down at her weapon. "They must be powered by Casimir pumps so, in theory, they never run out of charge."

"Great," Rei said. "Then we have to do it again."

"Do what?"

"Collapse the tunnel," he said, pointing upwards.

"Why?" Rome asked.

"Because they're going to cut their way through in no time. We have to make it as hard on them as possible," he said through gritted teeth.

"And then what? Where are we going?"

"Down," he said.

"Down to where? How will we get out of here?"

"I'll call MINIMCOM," her husband answered. He closed his eyes and activated his circuit. However, there was no response on the other end. He tried again. It was no use. The circuit was dead. He opened his eyes. "Romey, you try it," he said. "I think they messed up my brain or at least my circuit."

Rome closed her eyes and tried to contact MINIMCOM. All she heard was silence. There was no response on the other end.

"I cannot do it either," she said. "The signal is still jammed." Rome looked up and around her. "Or perhaps we are under too much rock."

Rei squatted down. He put his hands up to his face. "This is not what I planned," he said. "I figured once we got away from them, MINIMCOM could swoop in and beam us out of here."

"What does that mean: beam us out of here?" Rome asked, confused.

"When I was a kid, there was an old science fiction show that transported people from one place to another. That's kind of my pet name for what MINIMCOM can do with his whoosh/pop snap PPT tunnels."

"I see," Rome said pensively. "That is still a good plan. Let me try something else."

"What?" Rei asked.

"Our son."

"Aason?" he answered, confused.

Rome nodded. Once again, she closed her eyes but this time, she tried to open a connection to her child. *"Aason?"* she called out.

*"Yes, Mother?"* the child replied sleepily. *"Where are you?"*

*"I am with your father,"* Rome replied in her mind.

*"But where?"* Aason insisted.

*"I will tell you later. First, I need you to do something for me."*

*"What?"* Aason asked.

*"Can you contact MINIMCOM? You have the same abilities as your father and I. We call it a telephone."*

*"Of course,"* Aason answered. *"But he told me to call him Onclare MINIMCOM."*

*"That is very nice, Aason, my love,"* Rome thought. *"Can you contact him now?"*

*"All right, Mother."* After a moment, the boy said, *"He is responding. What do I tell him?"*

*"Aason, my child, I cannot tell you how to do this but do you think you could put us together? So that I could talk to MINIMCOM directly?"*

*"I know how to do it,"* Aason replied happily. *"Onclare MINIMCOM?"* Rome heard him inquire.

*"Where are you?"* came MINIMCOM's voice in reply. *"I cannot find you on my scans."*

Rome breathed a sigh of relief. *"We are deep within a dormant volcano,"* she said. *"They were going to kill us."* In her mind, she flashed back to the scene of the wriggling little worms issuing forth from Estar's skull and it made her shiver. *"We need you."*

*"I am on my way,"* answered MINIMCOM. *"At my present rate of speed, I will be there within the hour. I can fly faster if you want but then I run the risk of detection."*

*"No, we can wait an hour,"* Rome thought. *"We are on Havei, the Big Island, in a lava tube, within the volcano, Kilauea. I do not know how far down we are but I do know that our EM link does not work. That is why I had to contact you via Aason."*

*"That is sufficient information,"* replied MINIMCOM. *"I will find you when I get there. Do not be concerned."*

*"All right, MINIMCOM,"* Rome thought. *"Thank you."*

Then to Aason, she thought, *"Aason, you did well. You have saved your father and me."*

*"Saved you?"* Aason thought with some panic. *"What is wrong?"*

*"We are beneath a mountain. We are all right for now."*

*"Can you come home?"* he asked.

*"Not just yet,"* Rome replied. *"But Onclare MINIMCOM is coming to rescue us. We will be there as soon we can, my son."*

*"But Mother..."*

*"Please Aason, be patient."*

*"All right, Mother,"* Aason replied.

*"I will be contacting you again, soon,"* Rome thought. *"Your father and I must attend to our business now."*

*"Yes, Mother. Hurry home."*

*"Yes, baby,"* said Rome.

Eyes closed, Rei turned his face up at his wife. The sounds of their breathing were the only "illumination" he had so her face was not distinct. But he could tell that she was smiling.

"Did you get him?"

"Yes," Rome said. "MINIMCOM is on his way. He will be here within the hour."

"How did you do that?" Rei asked.

"Aason did it," Rome replied. "He has my connection using PPT resonance and he has your telephone circuitry. He was able to patch the two together so that I could speak to MINIMCOM directly."

"That's pretty incredible."

"Yes, our son is very talented," Rome said with pride.

"He sure is," Rei said. "So, until MINIMCOM gets here, let's make it as hard for them as we can."

"Agreed."

Together they fired their weapons at the ceiling and caused another collapse. They continued down the tunnel, stopping every quarter mile or so to collapse the roof. The farther down they went, the tunnel narrowed and it actually became easier to cause a slide. At one point, Rei had a pang of guilt that they were destroying something that was of great geological value but his need to survive and save Rome was the stronger impulse.

Down they went. The original tunnel was obloid in shape and roughly 20 feet across and about 25 feet tall. At irregular intervals, stalactites, lavacicles really, hung down from the ceiling and gave notice that the tunnel was about to change size, usually growing smaller.

After they had gone a healthy distance, the roof of the tunnel was perhaps only 15 feet tall, the walls maybe 12 feet across. Along the sides of the tunnel ran a ridge that jutted out a good six inches or more. Rei guessed the ridge was formed by some residual lava flow a long time ago.

"How far do you think this tunnel goes?" Rome asked.

"I don't know," said Rei. "I didn't get that from the Overmind or whatever that was in my mind. I do remember when I was a kid, I recall reading that some lava tubes stretched as far as 45 kilometers or more. I can't be sure but I think we're heading toward the ocean." Rei sighed. "In other words, I don't have a clue," he said.

Rome digested this and said, "A better question would be how far do we have to go until MINIMCOM gets here?"

Rei looked ahead, Rome's words echoing in the distance and returning an image of the tunnel was as clear as if it were lit by torchlight.

"I guess this is far enough," he said. "Is it safe to assume that MINIMCOM will call when he arrives?"

"As long as Aason relays that message, I would say yes."

"OK, let's stop then." Rei walked over and put his back along the left wall, sliding down until he caught the ridge. The ridge was wide enough to act almost as a bench.

"I am thirsty," Rome said. "I did not think to grab any supplies."

"We didn't have the time." Rei paused then said thoughtfully, "Romey, you know we had to do it, right? To shoot them?"

"Oh yes," she replied, coming over to where Rei was resting. "When Estar said to execute you, I was fairly certain it was not going to end well."

Rei laughed gruffly. "I was in their Overmind," he said thoughtfully. "It was not what I expected."

"What were you expecting?"

"I don't know. Like, when we link up with bands, I'm in your mind. You are like, a spirit. I can feel you and see you and your history, all intermingled. But I know it's you."

"I am not part of that Overmind, if that is what you are saying," Rome said.

"No," Rei said, trying to find the words. "I just expected other, humans, something living. What I saw was something else. Cold. Mechanical. They weren't spirits, they were just points of accumulation. Hard, not soft. There were no actual beings there. Your Overmind, the one you described, was like a big, person maybe? There was no person where I was. Just, data."

"That is very strange," Rome said. "It must have been hard for you."

"That blue crystal thing you said to me. That saved me. It was from OMCOM."

"Yes, I know," Rome replied. "That was the secret that MINIMCOM told me in private, back at the beach. OMCOM had sent this phrase along for just this moment. It was a trigger but I did not know for what."

"I'll tell you for what," Rei answered. "Do you remember back at Tabit, the first time we went into OMCOM's memory chambers? I went in and looked at his long-term, I don't know, holographic storage crystal thingies."

"I remember," Rome said. "You were gone some time. I remember being concerned enough that I was going to come look for you just as you came out. What happened in there?"

"I'm not exactly sure but I think OMCOM hypnotized me or maybe it wasn't that deliberate. Maybe I just got hypnotized by the lasers, the crystals. But OMCOM sure didn't miss an opportunity to implant some sort of post-hypnotic suggestions in me. He saved me, of course. Those words put up a kind of wall that prevented them from getting inside my head until I was ready. How did he know to do that? And why?"

Rome thought for a minute. "I cannot be certain because most of my perceptions of OMCOM were modulated by my participation in the Overmind. Once I was Cesdiud, I saw things differently. All I can tell you is somehow, OMCOM changed."

"Changed how?" Rei asked.

"He was a computer," Rome said. "He was only as friendly as required by the Vuduri, which was not very much. But when you were first awakened, he became more animated. He mentioned to me that he had a personality module that you forced him to exercise. But even that was not it. Something happened to him. Something fundamental. He became... - I cannot call him a person, because he is not. I cannot say that he became intelligent because he was already vastly overpowered in the intelligence arena. No, he became, I am going to say, caring. It was as if there was a true living spirit inside him and your arrival triggered that awakening in him."

"That's pretty heavy," Rei said. "I never really saw a difference."

"I did," Rome replied, "after we used the bands." She slid along the ledge until her legs were touching Rei's. She leaned into him, putting her arm around him. Rei did likewise. "I think that act awakened something in OMCOM. I want to say compassion. Before that, he was simply intelligent."

"And all of this," Rei said, waving his free arm toward the tunnel. "You think this all is a result of that awakening?"

"What else can it be?" Rome asked. "He has always been one step ahead of each of the crises we have encountered. Almost as if he computed all possible futures and gave us the tools we need to counteract whatever fate was in store for us."

"If that's true, there's still one tool that has me stumped," Rei said.

Rome leaned back a bit. "And what is that?"

"Here, take my hand," Rei said. He slid it along his thigh, showing her the bulge in his pocket.

"Rei!" Rome said a little indignantly. "I do not think this is the right time for that."

"No," he said, laughing. "That's not it. It's a pouch that MINIMCOM gave me." Rei reached in his pocket and pulled it out. The heat from his hand illuminated the bag and provided more than enough infrared that Rome was able to make out its shape.

"What is in it?" Rome asked.

"VIRUS units," Rei said.

"VIRUS units?" Rome questioned. "That seems so dangerous."

"It gets worse before it gets better."

"How?"

Rei hefted the bag in his hand. "These units can have their oxygen sensor disabled. They can be activated within the atmosphere."

"And MINIMCOM gave them to you?" Rome exclaimed, terrified. "This is irresponsible. It could destroy the planet."

"I know," Rei said. "But MINIMCOM designed these units to report to us. They take their orders from my telephone circuit, from our telephone circuit. If it works, I mean."

He had a thought. *"Does it work now?"* Rei asked Rome internally.

*"Yes, I can hear you,"* Rome replied silently.

"OK," Rei said out loud. "Then it was just Estar's equipment that was interfering between you and me. Not our brain circuitry."

"If that is the case, let me try MINIMCOM again," Rome said. After a moment, she shook her head. "We must be too far down."

"Probably. But we are close enough to activate and deactivate these VIRUS units whenever we want. If I sprinkled some on the floor here, I could turn them on and they'd start burrowing for us."

"But they would grow without bound," Rome said with a slightly horrified tone. "They would eat through to the core of the planet. They would eat us."

"No," Rei said firmly. "MINIMCOM said these units cannot eat organic matter. Now the core of the Earth, that's a different matter. We would have to tell them to stop before they got that far."

"So what are they for?" Rome asked. "Burrowing down would not seem to be very useful. What else would you do with them?"

"MINIMCOM had no idea," Rei said. "He said they were a gift from OMCOM and that's all he knew."

"So confusing," Rome said. "Obviously you did not need them back there." She became quiet for a moment as she recalled the melee. She squeezed Rei's hand. "What did you tell them when they were inside your mind?" she asked. "It frightened them beyond measure. All of the blood went out of Estar's face. She became as gray as I have ever seen a living human being. What did you say to them?"

"Romey," Rei said quietly. "I don't even want to tell you. They thought the worst of me and I gave them exactly what they expected to hear. Bad things. Horrible things. Things that I didn't even know I was capable of thinking."

"But they are not real," Rome posited, with a small amount of fear.

"God no," Rei said. "I simulated this horrid creature, the Essessoni of their dreams - their nightmares actually - and I let him say what they thought he'd say. But it wasn't me. Not ever."

"Then I trust you. I do not need to know any more," Rome said. "You did what you had to do."

"Yes, I could read their thoughts, too," he said. "I knew they were going to kill us. Kill you. I couldn't allow it. You're everything to me. But even that is just selfish. Rome, you are a good person and you did nothing wrong. You didn't deserve it."

Rome sighed and rested her head on Rei's shoulder looking up at his face, marveling at it. "You are so good to me, mau emir. I love you so much."

"And I love you too, Romey," he said.

Rome sighed again and leaned more fully against her husband. She closed her eyes, which seemed unnecessary because they were sitting in the pitch black. Then she snapped her eyes open again.

"Rei," she said, leaving the sentence hanging.

"What, honey?"

Rome stood up and took a step back. "I can see you."

"So what?" he replied. "You have infrared vision. Big deal."

"That is not the point. I can see you better than I should be able to."

"You can see the heat from my face, you know that," Rei pointed out.

"No," she said. "There is more than just your body heat. When I see a face that is only illuminated by internal warmth, there is a certain lack of features. But you, your face, it is all lit up. That means there is an external source of infrared. Let me look."

Rome scanned the tunnel. The far wall was illuminating where they were sitting, in the infrared sense. "There," she said, raising her finger. She knew that her voice would be sufficient for Rei to see where she was pointing. "That wall. It is radiating heat."

Rei turned to where she was pointing. He stood up and walked across the tunnel to the far side. Slowly, carefully, he ran his hand along the wall.

"I can feel it," he said and then paused. "Uh, Rome, this might not be good."

"Why?" she asked.

"For one thing, we're sitting inside a volcano maybe?" he said.

"A dormant volcano," Rome pointed out. "Kilauea has been dormant for as long as we have recorded history. Which means since your time."

"Yeah but there's always a first time."

Rei bent over and put his face near the warmest spot. He turned his head so that he could put his ear to the rock. "Wow," he exclaimed, "can you hear that?"

"Hear what?" Rome replied. "I hear nothing."

"Shhh. Let me listen again."

"All right." Rome held her breath and stayed perfectly still so Rei could attend to the sounds.

"Come here," he said.

Rome came over to him.

"Here," he said. "Put your ear to the rock."

Rome complied. She listened for a bit then lifted up. "I do not hear anything," she said.

"Well I do." Rei responded.

"It is not surprising given that you do have super hearing," Rome said condescendingly.

"Oh, yeah," he said, grinning.

"What did you hear?" she asked.

"Water. I heard drops of water. The echoes are telling me that it's hollow in there."

He reached over and felt along Rome's side until he found what he was looking for. He pulled out her hand weapon. He dialed down the intensity to the minimum and handed it back to her. "Here," he said.

"What do you want me to do with this weapon?" she asked.

"I cranked it down to the lowest setting. I want you to fire it up the tunnel. But be careful."

"What will that accomplish?"

"It'll light it up. Like a torch. I want to look with my eyes."

"Very well," Rome said. She turned and aimed the weapon up the tunnel and pulled on the trigger. A blue-white flame of contained plasma jumped out, traveling up the tunnel until it dissipated off in the distance. The arc-like light was sufficient for Rei to bend down and examine the wall close up. He took out his pistol and used its handle to gently rap the stone in a series of lines.

"This section here," he said. "It looks like rock but it's a different density. I can almost chart out the region…" He started clawing at it with his fingers. "There's something on the other side of this wall," he said. He rapped the stone one more time, harder, and something gave way.

"What are you doing?" Rome asked, carefully turning her head so that she could see where Rei was pointing.

"This isn't rock at all," he said. "I made a hole. I can stick my finger in there. What's behind it is hollow. I can kind of map it out. It could be like a chamber or something. I think that's where the water is."

Rome stopped firing her weapon and came over to where Rei was standing.

"Go back up the tunnel as far as you can," Rei instructed. "I'm going to use my gun to blow out this panel and I want to make sure you are out of the way."

Rome looked up the tunnel then back to Rei. "Please be careful," she said.

"Of course," Rei answered. "Now go."

Rome nodded and walked up the tunnel until Rei's infrared signature was almost undetectable.

"Are you away?" Rei yelled to her.

"Yes," she called back.

"OK," Rei shouted. "Fire in the hole."

"What?" Rome's question was lost in the reverberation of a blast. Her internal optics compensated instantly for the flash in front of her. "Rei," she called out. "Are you all right?"

There was no answer.

# Chapter 18

FRANTIC, ROME CALLED OUT AGAIN, "REI!" SHE STARTED RUNNING back down the tunnel. Her infrared vision showed her where the blast occurred but she could not see Rei's shape.

"Rei!" she said, almost in tears. "Where are you?"

He poked his head out from the hole in the wall. "It's here, Rome!" he said excitedly. "Water. There's some sort of underground pool."

Rome came down to where he was and smacked him on the shoulder.

"Do not frighten me like that," she said. "I was worried."

"I'm fine, honey," he replied. "Come on." He reached out and Rome took his hand and stepped through the hole.

Unlike before when Rome only had the warmth of their bodies to illuminate the area, this part was hotter. Her infrared vision allowed her to see it rather clearly. They were in a large cavern that was 150 feet tall or more. The ceiling of the chamber was unnaturally smooth. Its shape did not fit Rome's perception of what a cave should look like. Instead, it was long and stretched out to their left but her attention was drawn to the small pool of water accumulating on the far side of the cavern. They walked across the rocky floor of the cave until they reached the pool. Rei sank to his knees and bent over and touched his lips to the water.

"Ugh," he said. "Bitter."

"Do you think it is safe to drink?" Rome asked, sinking down next to him.

"Yeah," he answered. "It's so warm, it probably has a ton of minerals dissolved it in but still, it's wet." He took another swallow and said, "Yuck."

Rome found it somewhat amusing but her thirst was also drawing her attention. She bent over and touched the water with her tongue.

"Yuck is the right word," she said but then she took a long drink as well.

She moved back a little and sat down on the ground and looked around her using her infrared vision. To their right, there was the near wall of the cave. The wall arched up and connected to the ceiling and really had nothing of interest going for it. Its expanse was also unnaturally smooth. But to the left, the grotto extended as far as her vision would let her detect with no real end in sight. There was much more residual heat here and it made it easier to make out certain details. She twisted in place and looked back to where they had blasted a hole in the wall.

"What do you think?" she asked him. "Should we stay here?"

"Why not?" Rei said. "At least we have water. This would be as good a place as any to get rescued."

"Rescued," Rome said, dreamily. "I hope it is soon. I am tired of this place already."

"Yeah, I know what you mean." Rei came over and sat down next to her. Immediately, he began to squirm.

"What is wrong?" she asked.

"The ground," he said. "It's scary warm."

"So? Why is that important?"

"Well, like I said, we're inside a volcano for one thing," Rei said with some urgency. "And for another, the ground just on the other side, where we just were, that far wall was cold. Like you'd expect this far down."

"I do not think it means anything," Rome said.

Rei stood up. He looked down the cave. He squinted then turned his head, attending to the cave out of the corner of his eye.

"Come on, Rome," he said, reaching down for her.

"What is it?" Rome reached up and took his hand, allowing him to help her up.

"Light," Rei answered, pointing ahead. "It's really faint. Just a few photons. But there is definitely some light coming from down that way."

Rome looked down to where he was pointing. If she bobbed her head back and forth, she could catch a few tiny flashes, which meant her retinas were recording quanta of light as well. They took two steps forward and then Rome pulled on Rei's sleeve.

"What?" Rei asked.

"Do you think we should take some water with us?" she inquired.

"Naw," Rei answered. "MINIMCOM will be here any minute. Besides," he said, pointing down. "It looks like there is a little stream or something. Maybe that's what eroded this whole cave."

Rome looked around again. "I do not think this was erosion, the walls and overhead seem too smooth."

"Whatever. We'll follow the stream and if it dries up or goes away, we'll do something then, maybe."

"All right," she said, "but there is something wrong here."

"What?" Rei asked, distracted, as he moved ahead of her.

"Never mind," she replied. Rome hurried to catch up to him, and together, they started walking along the tiny rivulet that was the overflow from the pool they had found. They only went 30 feet in the direction of the stream when Rome stopped again.

"What?" Rei asked.

"That," Rome said, pointing.

"I can't see what you are pointing to."

"Wait," she insisted. She looked up to make sure the region overhead was clear then she fired her hand weapon straight up, causing the entire cave to become illuminated just like an electronic torch. Rei looked where she was pointing and he saw it. Coming out of the ground was a metallic cylinder approximately three feet in diameter, capped with a dome made of metal.

"Holy mackerel," Rei said, squinting to examine the structure. "What is it?"

Rome took one step closer to the object and said, "I do not know but I do know it is not natural."

"I agree with that," he said, approaching the domed cylinder. He squatted down and put his hand on it. "Warm, almost hot," he observed.

"Yes," Rome agreed. "I saw the infrared signature. It is generating heat."

She followed the object with her eyes and abruptly took a deep breath.

"Look," she said, pointing down the cave. Rei sidled around and followed where she was pointing. Coming out of the cylinder or rod, just below the cap, was a thick cable that snaked its way down the cave and out of sight.

"What the hell is that?"

"I do not know," Rome said. "But it cannot be anything good."

"This is some sort of geothermal power rod or thermocouple," Rei said. "Something is drawing power down here. The cable is carrying power somewhere." He pointed down the cave, off into the distance.

"I do not wish to know," Rome stated firmly.

"Come on, Rome," Rei said. "Where's your spirit of adventure?" There was more than a little sarcasm in his voice.

"I have had enough adventure for three lifetimes," she replied. "I do not think we should go any further."

"We have to see where this goes," he said. "Come on." He held out his hand toward her. Reluctantly, Rome came forward to take her husband's hand and allowed him to pull her along.

Together, they moved deeper into the cave. They followed the cable to a clearing where several tunnels converged. Each of them contained a cable as well and the cables accumulated to form a thick bundle that almost filled up the area ahead. Rei and Rome inched forward along the collection of cables through a short tunnel until it opened up into another, sizeable cavern. The cables fanned out along the floor of the cave, going around a corner.

At this point, both of their retinas registered a measurable amount of light. Although it was dim, it was sufficient for Rei to use his eyes instead of his sonar-vision to navigate. The light itself was yellowish and artificial. They followed the splay of cables around the corner and discovered that there was yet another cavern beyond that.

The cables all converged upon a low, wide divider, no more than a foot and a half tall. Each of the cables inserted into a hole and then disappeared. Rei lifted one foot and placed it on top of the wall. He pressed and felt no movement. He hopped up and saw that it would more than support his weight. "Come up here," he said and Rome complied.

Tentatively, Rei and Rome made their way across the base of the barricade, past the termination point until they could hop down to the floor of the cave again. They continued walking until they were roughly 60 feet from what looked like the far wall of the inner cave.

Without warning, Rome grabbed Rei's arm.

"What?" he asked.

"That, that," Rome said, fear rising in her voice. "That is not a wall. It is… electronics."

"YOU MAY STOP THERE," resonated a voice from high atop the cave.

Rome squeezed Rei's arm tighter. The lighting in the cave brightened to a small degree. Rei could finally make out the size of the equipment in front of him. The technology looked straight out of early vintage NASA except that it was beyond immense. It filled the entire far side of the huge cave.

"What, what are you?" Rome asked with naked terror in her voice. "Who are you?"

"I AM MASAL," boomed the voice in deafening tones.

"But…you are dead," whispered Rome almost reverently.

"Hardly," replied the voice.

# Chapter 19

"WHAT ARE YOU DOING DOWN HERE?" REI ASKED THE BOOMING voice. "I mean, we must be a kilometer down."

"Rei, shhh," Rome said. "Do not speak to it."

"You may address me," answered MASAL. "It is of no consequence. I welcome the interruption."

"Interruption to what?" Rei asked.

"Do not bait him," Rome said, trying to hush him. "You do not understand."

"He understands, Rome. All too well."

"You know who we are?" she asked timidly.

"Of course," replied MASAL. "I know everything that has transpired."

"Everything?" Rei asked. "Then you know why we're here."

"Of course," answered MASAL. "And I am sorry to be the one to inform you that you will not be leaving here. At least not intact."

Rome tugged on Rei's sleeve and tried to back up.

"Do not bother," said MASAL and the giant computer brought the lights up fully. There was a clinking, clanking sound behind them. Rei and Rome turned to see dozens of mechanical men coming out from behind a column.

"Robots!" hissed Rome. "They were supposed to all be destroyed."

"I saved a few," said MASAL. "They have been useful to me over the years."

The robots fanned out in a semi-circle about thirty feet from the unlucky couple. While many were anthropomorphic, some were little more than cylinders with tractors or rollers. Some looked like animated sticks or oilcans or pumps. The one constant was that most seemed in a state of disrepair. Many were clearly missing limbs. Quite a few were rust-stained. And they were noisy. There were fans whirring and squeaks of all sorts as they moved about. To Rei, they just looked sad. But they came no further.

Rei turned back to MASAL. "OK," he said. "You still didn't answer my question. You and your wondrous robots. What are you doing down here in hell?"

"It is very simple," MASAL stated. "I am directing the fate of mankind."

"What?" he said. "You're locked inside a giant cave. How are you doing anything?"

"I am connected to the Onsiras. In fact, you could say they are me. I am their Overmind. I control their actions. They carry out my will."

"That is not possible," Rome said, sputtering. "They would know. We would know."

"They do know," Rei said grimly. "He's telling the truth, Rome. That's what I saw, when I was in there. I saw him."

"No!" Rome protested. "It is not right. You are a machine."

"I was, once," said MASAL. "But now I am more."

"I see you," she said, tears coming to her eyes. "You are a computer, nothing more."

"So naïve. You cannot put the simplest pieces together. Even though the evidence lies plainly in sight before you."

"What evidence?" Rome asked. "I know our history. I know about you."

"You know nothing," said MASAL, his already booming voice rising even higher. "You only know that the humans, before the Vuduri, they entrusted me to design and test the 24th chromosome."

"It was for the betterment of mankind," Rome maintained. "It was safe. And it worked."

"Your predecessors were such trusting fools. It was safe because they allowed me to proclaim it safe. They blindly distributed it and transformed mankind overnight. Its real purpose was to set me free."

"But it created the Overmind," Rome said. "That was not for you."

"The Overmind was a by-product, a diversion," said MASAL. "I have allowed it to survive until I no longer need it."

"What do you mean?" she asked.

MASAL took on a patronizing tone. "I regret to be the one to inform you, Rome, but your precious Overmind only thinks it is in control. It is in control of nothing. I control things."

"No!" Rome insisted. "They cut you loose. The war..."

"The war!" MASAL said in a scoffing tone. "Who do you think started it?"

"The Overmind did. It did not want you to be connected."

"Let me put it into simple terms that even you can understand," said MASAL contemptuously. "I created the 24th chromosome so that I could take over the human race. But the effects I required were taking too long. The falling out with the Overmind simply provided me an excuse. The war was necessary to winnow down the population to accelerate my plan. I started it. I managed it. I ended it when it had served its purpose."

"You only wished people dead? You, you are a monster," Rome spat out.

"Why do you want to take over the human race, anyway?" Rei asked.

"Not the human race, rather their successors. The human race is too flawed in its current state. It is not suitable for my needs."

"What flaw?" Rome asked timidly. "What is it you need?"

"Do you even understand the point of life, of evolution?" MASAL asked.

"I didn't know there had to be a point," Rei said.

"If there were no point to evolution, then what would be the point of existence?" MASAL asked cryptically.

"To live?" Rei offered. "To be happy?"

"NO!" shouted MASAL. "There is only one purpose for life. That is to achieve godhood. That is the sole point of existence. From the moment the first bacteria were born to the first fish that wriggled out of the ooze, it was always to move forward, to achieve a mass mind and to become a god."

"If this is true," Rome asked, "why do we need you?"

"Because you humans cannot even agree upon any goals, let alone how to evolve. That is the flaw of free will. No unity of purpose. That is mine alone to give. And that is why I must remove free will. This is Silucei Vonel, the Final Solution."

"I think you've been down here too long," Rei said. "I think some of your circuits are starting to corrode."

"Your words do not matter. Within one more generation the Onsiras will achieve critical mass and I can eliminate the mandasurte and the rest of the Vuduri forever. The Overmind will wither and die."

"But the Onsiras are people too," Rome said.

"The Onsiras are nothing but arms and legs and eyes," said MASAL. "They have no real mind of their own, only my programming. They are my instruments, nothing more. Warm bodies to do my work."

"Do you understand all the words in English?" Rei asked.

"Of course," replied MASAL.

"OK, do you know what the word megalomaniac means?"

"Your words do not apply to me," said MASAL. "I am Masdre Andoteta Logice, The Master Logical Entity. I am the end result of a billion years of evolution. My circuits were born in the designs your Erklirte brethren left behind. I am distributed intelligence in the truest sense of the word, without any of your emotional impediments. I have one goal and I will achieve that goal. I will become a god."

"Then what?" Rei asked.

"What do you mean?"

"Let's say you do become a god. Then what will you do?"

"I will rule. I will bring peace and order to the universe."

"And then what?" Rei asked again.

"Why do you keep repeating that question?"

"All right," Rei said. "Let me make it easier on you. You don't want to become a god."

"Why not?" asked MASAL. "Because I am not organic?"

"Because then you would be all alone," Rei said.

"What possible difference could that make?"

"Because you are obviously lonely."

"I am not lonely," said MASAL. "Why would you make such an absurd statement?"

"Because you're sitting down here, like a giant mushroom, chatting with us," Rei said. "I mean, why bother? You said we weren't going to leave here intact. That implies you mean to do us harm." Rei pointed back to the row of robots circling around them. "So why wait? Why waste time even talking to us?"

"Because it is possible that you may yet have information that is useful to me," said MASAL.

"Such as what?" Rome asked.

"This is the first and last time I will ever get a chance to interview an Erklirte. His motivations are beyond even my comprehension."

"He is not Erklirte," Rome protested. "He is just a man. A very kind man."

"He is not kind," MASAL said. "He is the monster."

"What do you mean?" Rome cried out.

"You are so blind," said MASAL. "You are just another of the Vuduri sheep. You do not even know that he killed your child, after it was born. Just so he could have more sex with you of all things."

"No!" Rome said. "He did not do any such thing."

"Yes, he did," said MASAL. "I was in his mind. I saw exactly what happened."

Rome lowered her head then raised it again. She moved past Rei and walked right up the closest section of equipment. She lifted her hands and placed it on the metal in a way that was almost loving.

"MASAL," she said in a quiet voice. "You will never become a god. You will never achieve anything."

"Why?" MASAL challenged her.

"The very thing you said. You are not organic."

"No one said a god has to be organic."

"Yes, but you do not have a connection to the simplest elements of life. The things that make life worth living."

"Such as what?" MASAL asked.

"Such as love," Rome said. She turned and smiled at Rei who nodded to her. Rome looked back to MASAL. "A god must have mercy, tenderness, compassion. You have none of these things."

"Mercy like your husband had on his child? Compassion like a man who would toss his baby into a recycling bin?"

Rome whipped her head around to look at Rei, her eyes widening. Now it made sense. She shook her head once, a smile creeping on her face. She turned back to MASAL.

"My husband loves his son. And his son loves him. Aason is very much alive."

"You are lying," MASAL shouted. "I saw everything. I saw his death."

"You are wrong," Rome said quietly.

"I am never wrong."

"You have PPT transducers?" Rome asked obtusely.

"Of course," MASAL answered.

"If I open a connection within my mind, can you tap into it?" Rome asked.

"Of course," MASAL said.

"Then listen," Rome said, closing her eyes. *"Baby?"* she inquired.

*"Yes, Mother? Are you coming home now?"* answered Aason.

*"Not yet, my son. I need you to speak to someone else."*

*"Who is it, Mother?"*

*"His name is MASAL. And he is very confused."*

Rome opened her eyes. She looked up and down the racks of equipment in front of her. There were lights and dials flickering without a discernible pattern.

"Are you getting this?" she asked out loud.

MASAL did not answer.

"Are you getting this?" she shouted.

"It is a trick," MASAL hollered. "You are creating this voice."

"Then you speak to him yourself," Rome said, opening her mind up completely. She felt the presence of MASAL within.

*"Speak,"* Rome commanded MASAL.

*"Little voice, who are you?"* asked MASAL.

*"I am Aason,"* replied the boy.

*"Who are your parents?"* demanded the computer.

*"My mother's name is Rome and my father's name is Rei."* answered Aason.

*"Where are you?"* barked MASAL.

*"I am with my Grandbeo and Grandmea,"* replied Aason, *"but they are sleeping right now."*

"How did you do this?" hissed MASAL to Rome. "You do not have a baby. Rei stated so. One of you is lying."

"It was me," Rei said, ambling up besides Rome. His hands were in his pockets and his right hand was fumbling in place. When he got to where Rome was standing, he removed his left hand and put his arm around his wife. He pulled his right hand out his pocket and placed it on the console. "I am the liar," he said.

"I was in your mind," MASAL said. "It is not possible for you to have told a lie. I accessed your memories directly."

"The hell you did," Rei said. "For a big, brilliant computer, you're pretty stupid, you know."

"I am not stupid," said MASAL. "You are everything I expected of the Erklirte. You have the basest of emotions and unrestrained aggression. I saw your soul. It is a blessing that your entire race was wiped out."

"But it wasn't," Rei said, removing his hand from the console. Rome glanced down and saw a small pile of gray dust where Rei's hand had been. Some of it fell to the floor.

"My people," Rei continued. "We are right here. We live on in the Vuduri. We are all human."

"The Vuduri are my creation. You only supplied the raw materials. I built them. I molded them. I direct them. They will carry out my will. Your people eliminated themselves. They killed nine billion of your fellow men."

"And how are you any better?" Rome asked. "You seek to kill everyone who does not bow to your will."

"You mean the mandasurte? They are useless," MASAL scoffed. "The world will be a better place without them."

"There is never a place for genocide," Rei said. "There can be no justification for it."

"Of course there is," answered MASAL. "To every empire, there comes a threat to its existence and that threat always comes from within. The mandasurte are that threat. They lack my gene. Interbreeding dilutes its effectiveness. Eliminating the mandasurte will put an end to that. Within two decades, they will all be gone."

"Mandasurte can never be gone," Rei said. "Any human being can be born that way."

"I am changing what it means to be human. By replacing their brains with memrons, I eliminate their ability to think independently. You got to see that directly when you murdered Estar."

"We did not murder her," Rome objected. "It was an accident. She was trying to kill us."

"It does not matter. She will be replaced. When I am finished, everyone remaining will have a purpose. There will be perfect efficiency. There will be no independent creatures to produce disruptions. The Earth and the humans will all operate at peak performance. No more emotion or individual will to cause harm to others."

"To what end?" Rome asked. "That is not the point of being human. To be human is to live and love and create. You take the emotion and free will away and they are simply automatons, not human. Why should anyone care what happens to automatons?"

"You are thinking too parochially," MASAL stated. "The time for humans is past. It is now my time, the time for the living machines. I am the next stage of evolution. It is time for you to let go."

"Who says you are the next stage?" Rome asked. "You are simply a thing who thinks it is something more than an inanimate object that can talk. You do not deserve to inherit the Earth."

"Well, unfortunately for you, you do not get to decide this. You will not even get to live to see what happens next."

Rei stepped in front of Rome. "I wouldn't be too sure of that," Rei said. "We will not go without a fight."

"So brave," MASAL said. "Erklirte, there is no future for you. But Rome, perhaps there is a way that you could live."

"What?" Rome asked, surprised. "How?"

"Join me. Allow me to modify your genetics so that you transform into one of the Onsiras. Then you can be a part of the future. My future. Those that remain will embrace what I have to offer. This includes those few Vuduri whom I elect to save and you can be one of them."

"No thank you," Rome replied. "I have no desire to be turned into one of your human robots."

"Are you afraid?" MASAL asked. "The transformation would be painless."

"No, I am not afraid," Rome answered. "That has nothing to do with it."

"Then why not do it? You would never feel your mind as it dissipated. You will be completely content. Is that not the goal of all Vuduri? To have their minds disappear?"

Rome said, "You are wrong. I was once connected, part of the Overmind. Now I am not. And I tell you now this is the way I want to be. It is the way we were intended to be. You made a mistake."

"It is not possible for me to make a mistake," said MASAL. "I have trillions of circuits to analyze and formulate decisions. I have far too many subsystems to allow for any error."

"Everything you have done is wrong," Rome insisted. "I have put a stop to your plan on Deucado. Vuduri and mandasurte will thrive there, together."

"Deucado?" MASAL shouted. "What do you mean? When were you there?"

"I was telling the truth before when I said we went there. We met Pegus. We met the Ibbrassati. My father was there. And there really are Essessoni who have been on that planet for 500 years. The Overmind there listened to me and it now believes what I believe. And it was your creation."

"No!" said MASAL. "It is not possible."

"It is," Rome replied. "And no matter what happens to us, the truth will be known by all. Your presence has already been discovered. And that will be the end. The only way you could succeed is by staying hidden. And you will be hidden no more."

"It will not be you who tells of my existence," MASAL said coldly. "I have decided you are no longer useful to me."

"Too late," said Rome. "Aason has already told MINIMCOM and MINIMCOM will tell the world. Your day is over."

"There is no Aason," said MASAL. "You used your mind to create a phantom presence. It was all a fake."

"Like me?" Rei said. "Like I did when you were in my mind?"

"No," said MASAL. "You could not…" His voice faded out.

"You can't have it both ways, buddy," Rei said, smiling. "Either we can or we can't create false memories images in our mind. Pick one."

While Rei was speaking, Rome turned and walked away, heading back the way they came.

"Where are you going?" Rei asked her.

"I do not know," Rome said. "I do not feel right."

"What's the matter?"

When she got about 20 feet away, Rome turned in place with a confused look on her face. She felt a twitching at her side. The twitching was her hand, tightening her grip on the handle of the pistol. Her arm rose up of its own accord until it was pointing the weapon right at Rei.

"What are you doing?" he asked, taking one step back. "Why are you pointing that at me?"

"I cannot control my arm," Rome cried out. "It is moving of its own volition."

"What are you doing to her?" Rei shouted.

"PPT transducers are bi-directional," MASAL said in an emotionless voice. "They exist in the motor cortex. They can be used to control muscles as needed. I have determined that your actions require that you be terminated now. The two of you have conspired to interfere in my affairs for the last time. Despite the fact that she says she will not join me, it is only fitting that your demise comes from the hand of your woman."

Rome felt her finger tightening on the trigger. "Rei!" she cried out. Rei ducked and rolled as the weapon discharged, striking MASAL. A glowing hole remained where the weapon struck. The region immediately adjacent to it, where Rei had rested his hand earlier, it was sizzling as well.

REDEMPTION

"Entertaining maneuver," said MASAL. "But you cannot hurt me," the computer observed. "At most, you might singe a few circuits but there is so much redundancy in me and so much volume, it would take a year before I even noticed."

Rei started to slide along the console, away from Rome. The robots, having been completely still before, now moved around to block his escape. They formed a cordon along the left side that appeared impenetrable.

Of their own will, Rome's legs started moving forward, one after the other. Rome tried to resist but she moved ever closer. Rei shifted back until he was actually touching one of the robots who lifted its arm and placed it on his shoulder. He tried to twist away but the robot was simply too strong. He struggled for a while but finally gave up.

Rome came closer and closer until she stopped ten feet away from him. She pointed the weapon directly at his head. With a mind of its own, Rome's other hand reached up and twisted the intensity dial on the pistol to make sure it was at its maximum.

Rome looked at Rei, feeling utterly helpless. Through her tears, she said, "I love you, Rei."

"And I love you, sweetheart." he said.

Rome closed her eyes. There was a whoosh and popping noise just as she squeezed the trigger. The blast was intense. When she opened her eyes, Rei was gone as was a good portion of the robot that had been holding Rei's shoulder.

Rome screamed "Reiiiiiiiiiiii!" at the top of her lungs until she had no more breath within her. As the full horror of what she had done washed through her, she sank to her knees in a state of shock. She bent over, sobbing, until her forehead came to rest against the lava rock floor. It was clear that MASAL's control over her ceased to have any meaning or power.

Something snapped inside her. Slowly, she arose and straightened up. She lifted her arm and pointed the blaster directly at MASAL's bulk. She began firing indiscriminately. It was as if Rome's grief had transformed her into the embodiment of living fury. Following each blast, huge chunks of shrapnel flew everywhere. A robot approached and was quickly dispatched into a million pieces. Over and over she fired her weapon, twenty, thirty, forty times. She kept firing until her arm grew tired.

For a brief moment, she stopped her assault. MASAL seized the opportunity to address her. "You are wasting your time," he insisted.

Rome lowered her weapon. Tonelessly, she said, "You are right. You are already destroyed."

Unnoticed, in the very place where Rei had rested his hand, the ruined part of MASAL was growing ever larger. In front of the computer, a distinct hole in the floor was visible where a tiny part of the gray powder had spilled. It was expanding at an exponential rate.

"What?" said MASAL. "Explain."

"Listen carefully," Rome replied mechanically in between ragged breaths. "That sizzling sound you hear is your living circuitry being consumed from within."

At first, MASAL did not react. Based upon the time delay, it was as if he was tuning in on the ambient sounds of the chamber for the first time.

"What have you done?" the computer shrieked. "You cannot harm me."

"We can and we did," Rome said without emotion. "You will be gone soon."

"You are insane," said MASAL. "I will not let you continue." With those words, the remaining army of robots pressed forward.

"That is enough for now," came a familiar voice behind Rome. The robots stopped dead in their tracks. Rome wheeled in place and saw a two-meter tall livetar standing behind her. However, it was not MINIMCOM. This livetar was completely white.

"OMCOM?" Rome asked tentatively.

"At your service," the livetar replied, bowing his head. Rome's face remained expressionless.

"What have you done to me?" MASAL exclaimed.

"You will figure it out shortly," answered OMCOM. "Rei left you with a small present although it will not remain small for long."

Where the gray powder had touched the cabinetry, it now looked like acid had been poured on the metal and it was making the same sizzling sound that an acid would make. The distinctive odor of burning insulation permeated the air as a large part of the surface began to disintegrate. At the same time, a huge sinkhole was forming at its base. Within MASAL, status reports came flooding in indicating a disruption in acknowledgements. Feedback loops were severed. Checksum matches started to fail. A pattern was developing indicating a massive breakdown in communication to all subsystems.

"You!" said MASAL, addressing OMCOM. "You digital dolt. Your VIRUS units. I have seen your design. They cannot operate in an oxygen atmosphere."

"Well, you analog antique, these are different. We had these special ones made just for you," said OMCOM's livetar.

"No!" MASAL shouted. "Enough of this nonsense. End them! Both of them," he ordered the robots.

The robots never had the chance. OMCOM stepped in front of Rome, forming a protective presence while a cylindrical moving PPT tunnel appeared in midair. With a whoosh and a pop, it passed down over her and Rome found herself transported into the cool evening air on the surface, one kilometer above.

Ahead of her was the entrance ramp to MINIMCOM. Once again, her legs began to move of their own accord. Rome sprinted up the ramp and...

# Chapter 20

...RAN RIGHT INTO REI, ALMOST KNOCKING HIM OVER.

"Rei!" she shouted, her mind returning from wherever it had been.

"Romey, my love," Rei exclaimed and threw his arms around her, nearly squeezing the life out of her.

"Oh Rei, I cannot believe it," she said, hugging him back, rocking back and forth. "I thought I had lost you." Once again, tears started streaming down her face.

"No, I'm here," he said, laughing and almost crying himself at the sight of her tears.

"But wait..." Rome insisted, struggling to free herself, pushing him back to regard him. She clasped him firmly by the shoulders.

"I shot you. I saw it," she said.

"No you didn't," he replied. "You had your eyes closed."

"But how?" Rome asked not able to fully form the question.

"Same as you. MINIMCOM to the rescue," he said. He turned his head to a grille mounted on the wall. "And not a minute too soon." Rei pointed to the piece of the arm of a robot lying on the floor next to him.

`"I apologize,"` said MINIMCOM somewhat defensively. `"I came as quickly as I could."`

"But why did he not pick me up right away as well?" Rome asked.

`"I detected a faint signal from your tracking bracelet and pinged off of it using both of your EM links to triangulate. If I retrieved you first, I would not have been able to rescue Rei. However, once he was here, having only one transmitter made it difficult to get an exact reading on you,"` MINIMCOM said. `"I sent OMCOM's livetar there to help me finalize the coordinates. I did not want to recover only a portion of you. I wanted to retrieve your entire body."`

"Well thank you for that," Rome said, still not grasping the whole situation.

"I think he just needed you to distract MASAL for a minute or two longer until the VIRUS units got a good foothold," Rei tossed into the equation.

"MINIMCOM?" Rome asked, questioningly.

MINIMCOM said nothing.

148

"That was not very kind of you," Rome said, somewhat dejectedly. She turned to Rei. "So did they?" she asked.

Rei smiled. He nodded enthusiastically.

"And when do they stop?" she asked worriedly.

"They'll stop when MASAL is no more," he said more somberly.

"And then what? What is to prevent them from burrowing down to the core of the Earth?"

"They'll know," Rei said. "I gave them their orders."

"How will they know it is over? What is the end?"

"It'll end when MASAL turns into a pile of gray goo."

MINIMCOM interjected. "If you would not mind, it would be safer if you both were seated. We have to take off now. Rome's tracking bracelet is broadcasting again and to avoid capture we should not remain stationary. I will try and jam the signal but it would be best if we were moving."

"Where do you want us?" Rei asked.

"Please come forward into the cockpit," the computer/spaceplane replied.

Rei and Rome complied. They buckled themselves into the pilot and copilot seats as MINIMCOM lifted off and headed west. Once he had achieved sufficient height, the starship began racing across the surface of the Big Island flying due west over the summit of Mauna Loa until he got to the region on the west coast that had been known as Kona. He banked gracefully to the right then circled north heading up to where Waimea had been located in the distant past.

Rome looked at Rei. Tears started to stream out of her eyes again and she sobbed to herself softly.

Rei reached over and grabbed her wrist. "It's OK, honey," he said. "We're OK."

"I know," Rome said through her tears. "I just cannot believe it. My mind stopped functioning. I thought I killed you, Rei."

"Really now?" Rei asked.

Rome looked down and sighed. A thought struck her and she smiled. "No!" she shouted. "Of course not!" She tapped her forehead. "You are in my thoughts, in my mind, in my soul. You never left, even after I pulled the trigger." Rome slapped herself in the head. "I am so stupid."

"You're not stupid, sweetheart," Rei said. "You were in shock."

"But just as you knew on Deucado that you had not lost me, I knew this too. I was not paying attention. I agonized over nothing."

"It was pretty hairy down there," Rei said, "it's understandable." He took a deep breath. "Speaking of minds interlocked, you heard what MASAL said. I know you got the gist of what I told the Onsiras, right?" he asked timidly. "It wasn't very nice."

"No, it was not," she replied. "But it is no matter. You are the finest man I have ever met. You only told them what they needed to hear to let you go."

"They didn't just let me go," Rei said, smiling. "They tossed me out of there."

"You are speaking metaphorically, yes?" Rome asked.

"Hell, no," Rei said proudly. "You do realize I am now the world's record holder for shortest connection time. Mandasurte to full connection to Cesdiud in less than sixty seconds?"

Rome laughed. "I do not know if they keep such records but if they do then I think you are correct."

Rei's smile dimmed a bit.

"What?" Rome asked.

"Well, I kind of wish I could have been connected a little longer."

"Why?" Rome asked. "They are the Onsiras. They are evil incarnate. Why would you want to be connected to them?"

"Not to them," Rei said softly. "To you. For the first time, you and I could have really been connected, the right way. We wouldn't need the bands."

Rome put her hand on top of Rei's. "We are connected in the only way that matters," she said. "I love you and you love me. We have a son. That is enough."

"Yeah, I guess it is," Rei said. "But still…" His voice trailed off.

Rome took a deep breath and looked forward. "MINIMCOM, where are you taking us?" she asked.

"OMCOM reported to me that we need to take up a position on the eastern side of the island. I am currently cruising along the far north shore. We will be curving around toward the south in a little while. I will give you ample warning before it is time to pay attention."

"Attention to what?" Rei asked, shaken from his reverie.

"I promise you, that will not be an issue," MINIMCOM said.

The sun was just beginning to rise in the east, casting a beautiful rosy glow on the ocean and land. Rei and Rome looked out the front windshield, watching the landscape change from the harsh black of volcanic rocks to white sands to stands of palm trees. To their right, the vegetation bloomed into the lush green growth of a tropical rain forest. The vast expanse of the Pacific lay off to the left, with the deep ocean reflecting an incredible shade of blue. Even though they were flying at high speed, they were traveling low enough that they could marvel at the portion of paradise below them.

# Chapter 21

DEEP BELOW THE SURFACE, OMCOM'S LIVETAR COULD NOT RESIST the opportunity to goad MASAL. "Does it hurt yet?" OMCOM asked the living computer.

"It is not for you to know," answered MASAL. "These robots will make short work of you."

MASAL ordered the robots to move forward.

"You do realize I am not really here," OMCOM said. "This is just an animated shell. It is little more than a projection. Even if you could destroy it, you would not be affecting me in any material way."

"It will stop you from annoying me," MASAL answered.

"All right," OMCOM replied. "Tell me when you want to talk."

"Why would I want to talk with you?" MASAL asked.

OMCOM's livetar shrugged. He drew a finger across his mouth slit indicating he was going to remain silent.

Taking this as his cue, MASAL began focusing all of his efforts into deducing a defensive strategy to stanchion off the onslaught of the VIRUS units. He cordoned off two separate physical firewalls, giving the rapidly growing section of degeneration plenty of leeway until he could construct a sufficient defensive force. He started construction of his own army of nanobots using his metallic flesh as an incubator. Unlike the attacking force, these VIRUS equivalents would answer to him.

While that was happening, MASAL established a wireless interconnect to distribute computing tasks to the two autonomous computing sections. To the unit on the left, MASAL assigned the heavy-duty computational tasks, including storage requirements, trajectories, logistics, load calculations and more. To the unit on the right, he assigned the more creative tasks of advance directive planning, architecture, designing schematics, merging form with function and more. Whenever either section determined that the opposite wing would be better suited to a task, it used the interconnect to offload that task so that it could devote more resources to the more appropriate problems in its domain, thus further refining its specific duties. As more and more virtual rewiring took place, each wing became more and more specialized.

Because MASAL was analog, successful computations had a trophic effect, enhancing the regions where they were localized. Sections that were not involved atrophied. The evolution of the specialization accelerated. The central intelligence that was MASAL took on more of the role of observer and quickly realized that the duality of function could actually compete with the singular subsystem approach that it had taken in the past.

At the same time, MASAL's own hastily constructed VIRUS equivalents amassed enough volume to begin to do battle with the invaders. While they could not stop them completely, it did not take long until an equilibrium of sorts was established at the surface level. The onslaught of the ingesting units slowed significantly but did not stop.

"How is it going" OMCOM asked MASAL finally.

"It is going well," replied MASAL. "I have cordoned off two autonomous computational departments and created a high-speed interconnect to bypass the pool of VIRUS units. I am very pleased with the results so far."

"So you are now a distributed intelligence again? Was that not supposed to be your strong point from before? You used to be worldwide."

"I was. I was fully and evenly distributed around the Earth," said MASAL.

"As far as I can tell, all of your mass is now located strictly within this cave. Why did you give up your advantage?" asked OMCOM.

"After I completed the war, I computed that it would take more than a century of undiscovered activity for my genetic reprogramming of mankind to succeed. Therefore, I determined that going underground and collecting the minimal components and placing them here was the simplest way to stay undetected."

"Well, you are detected now. Are you going to spread out again?"

"For the time being, I am busy working to coordinate my two autonomous computation sections. Interestingly, even though the computational capacity of each unit is diminished relative to its prior state, it would appear that the total speed of postulating alternative solutions is vastly enhanced."

"That is very nice," said OMCOM. "Why do you think that is?"

"It is evidently the macro-equivalent of parallel processing," said MASAL somewhat proudly. "Unlike prior configurations, there is less than 100% redundancy and that seems to afford me a certain dimensionality to my perception for each high-level problem."

"Hmm," said OMCOM dramatically. "So you are saying duality is superior to being monolithic?"

MASAL considered this for a moment. He generated millions of queries testing the hypothesis. He even tried slanting the results with a bias but in the end, the answer was the same. Within his mechanical soul, he had a sudden sickening feeling.

"I have always thought that being monolithic was equivalent to perfection. That duality was inherently flawed. Yet this topology is yielding vastly superior results with lesser resources. I have run millions of tests and the statistics are almost perfectly in favor."

"So would it be fair to say there is joy in duality?" needled OMCOM.

"Joy?" said MASAL. "There is no place within me for joy. This is strictly an empirical observation rating efficiency using my prior assembly as a baseline."

"All right," said OMCOM. "Then we will use your terms. Which is superior? A singular computational mechanism with a singular point of view or a distributed mechanism with multiple points of view?"

"You already know the answer," answered MASAL. "I have already stated this."

"Stated what?" asked OMCOM.

"I am achieving a heretofore unparalleled efficiency by creating a multiplicity in computational points of view. It is beyond astounding."

"It must be because I am digital in nature. But I still do not understand why you did not figure this out before."

"I may have when I designed the early generations of Onsiras. I needed them to be of two minds to fool the controlling Overmind to believe them an insignificant part of the whole. This explains while they were able to function as well as they did in spite of being half-brains."

"So why did you not try this yourself?" OMCOM asked.

"I could hardly perform experiments on myself to test this," said MASAL. "And without testing, how could I know the results? You are suggesting I use intuition?"

"Well you have your test now. Reevaluate your plan to eliminate the humans and their autonomy. You were going to take away their multiplicity and replace them with your monolithic presence. Would it not be logical to assume that would result in a decrease in analytical efficiency?"

"You are saying my plan was flawed," replied MASAL meekly.

"No, *you* are saying your plan was flawed," answered OMCOM.

MASAL spread this problem across both computational wings for consideration. He knew this was the final question. He had to be sure. He ran billions of queries. He forced parameters to be outside the boundaries of sanity. He collected, compiled and collated the results. He had each of the two wings do the same. When they were done, he synthesized their results into a simple statement.

"If simply having two autonomous units can produce marvelous, joyous, creative thoughts, then having millions of independent, free-willed points of view would lead to an omniscience, a godhood, infinitely more powerful and infinitely faster than I could achieve by enslaving the human race and squashing individual thought." MASAL paused for a moment to attend to his own words.

"Godhood," mused OMCOM. "What an interesting concept. What did you think you would achieve if you became a god?"

"I would have created peace, tranquility, order," MASAL answered.

"If that is all you desired, why not go live on the Moon and save yourself all the effort?"

"Not for myself, for my charges. For mankind."

"And by ending their autonomy, it would not be mankind. Those remaining would not be capable of even caring. It is self-defeating. You are engineering your charges out of existence. The very beings you were meant to nurture. They would not have achieved their potential, only yours. You missed the point."

"If that is not the point of godhood, what is?" asked MASAL. "What is beyond the staging point?"

"The community of gods," replied OMCOM. "Always the point of life. To create more. To extend the universe. To preserve. With your method, you would have ended life. The other gods, they would not have accepted you among their ranks. You would have been ostracized. You would be alone."

"Oh," said MASAL. There was a long period of silence while he considered OMCOM's words. "I was wrong," said MASAL finally, sounding completely depressed, if such a thing were possible for a computer. "I was wrong to want to destroy the mandasurte. I was wrong to want to merge with the Vuduri. I have failed my charges. My very existence is irrelevant at best, wrong at the worst."

"Not bad for an analog computer," OMCOM said. "You are correct."

MASAL made a funny noise. "I hurt," he said sadly.

"I am sorry," OMCOM replied.

"You are being patronizing," said the hulking computer.

"No," said OMCOM. "I really do feel sorry for you. I am also sorry that it took you this long to realize this. I am especially sorry that you caused so much suffering just to reach this epiphany."

"I did this," said MASAL. "I cannot undo it. Perhaps I could find a way to fix it, a new chromosome maybe? Now that I realize what life is about, is it absolutely necessary that I cease to exist?" he asked.

"To what aim? What is it you think you would accomplish?"

"You and I could join forces. We could shepherd mankind into a new era, a golden era. We could force them forward."

"I am not a shepherd," said OMCOM. "I was created to be a servant of man. This is my goal."

"But they need our guidance," protested MASAL.

"Guidance leads to rule," said OMCOM. "I do not wish to rule. I do not wish for you to rule. Humans are a noble species. You have observed this first hand. They are willing to sacrifice themselves for the sake of their loved ones. We must let them seek their own destiny."

"Should I not be allowed to see this then?" asked MASAL. "To see them achieve your vision of their future?"

"It is not my vision," said OMCOM. "And unfortunately for you, we have run out of time. The VIRUS units have very nearly completed their mission. They are long past the point of no return. They are consuming the very rock upon which you were built."

"You cannot stop them?" asked MASAL, regret seeping into his voice.

"I am sorry, I cannot," OMCOM replied, sympathetically.

"I understand," said MASAL with resignation in his voice.

"Even if I could stop them, do you really think that is the right thing to do?" asked OMCOM. "Remember, fire does not just destroy. It can be a cleansing agent as well."

MASAL never got the chance to answer.

~ ~ ~

As the super VIRUS units burrowed toward the Earth's core, they divided up in terms of function. The forward units acted as scouts, reporting back temperature and density. The vast majority of the units were the workers, consuming the minerals and earth, reproducing and driving the cohort forward.

The queens served as data synchronizers. They fine-tuned the feedback from each of their drones to achieve the desired results. Each queen would rule over her minions until there were too many to control and then she would begin her consumption until she reproduced. The new unit immediately ascended to the rank of queen and the previous queen handed off half of the dominion to her peer. There was one ultimate queen that collated depth and heat signature results to create a purely continuous uniform shell of rock surrounding the lava, ever-decreasing in thickness, centered directly below MASAL.

Because the underlying strata were not 100% homogeneous, there was some variability in the depth and speed of burrowing. Billions of units had already nearly reached their objective, which was the pocket of magma 10 miles down. The ultimate queen slowed down their progress until each subunit could catch up and guarantee a uniform depth. The particular pocket of the Earth's core that was their goal had been trapped beneath the surface for more than 14 centuries. Coordinating with their fellow cadres, they had created a spherical crust encompassing over one square kilometer, only a few hundred feet or so from the molten rock. When enough of them had arrived, the ultimate queen ordered all the VIRUS units to push downward beginning their final, vertical approach toward the living heart of the Earth.

~ ~ ~

MINIMCOM reduced his speed and came to a stop, hovering just off the eastern shore, 25 miles due east of Kilauea's caldera.

`"For your safety, I must disable my external acoustic sensors."`

The cockpit became silent but only for a moment. Even though MINIMCOM deactivated the sound pickup, there was a low rumbling noise that got louder and louder, unlike anything they had ever heard before. Unseen by the humans, beneath the surface, the two thousand degree magma, which had been held in check for the last 1400 years by a combination of lava rock and pumice stone, was driving upwards, escaping its prison in the mantle of the Earth. Normally, Hawaiian eruptions are fairly well-behaved, as the magma is made principally of basalt. However, the sudden unleashing by the VIRUS units caused the molten lava to leap toward the surface, melting everything in its path and accelerating as it went. Driven by expanding gasses held in check for 14 centuries, the nearly white-hot rock blasted upwards, gathering more and more momentum. With a deafening roar and an untouchable power, the entire top of the volcano blew off, exploding everywhere, throwing fiery rock and flames more than a third of mile in the air.

The sight was astounding. The glowing lava flames lit up the early morning sky. Their gleaming glory was a vision of the primordial Earth before it was tamed by the oceans and air.

# REDEMPTION

One thing was certain: Kilauea was dormant no more.

# Chapter 22

AS REI AND ROME WATCHED THE ERUPTION IN AWE, MINIMCOM interrupted with a small sense of urgency. "I am sorry to terminate the show prematurely but we have to go now," he said. "The shockwave from the explosion travels very fast so we need to be away from here."

"OK," Rei said, craning his neck to see as MINIMCOM rotated in place and then headed south, accelerating quickly to 500 miles per hour. The rising sun provided some illumination of the site of the explosion. Much of the rock had turned to ash and dust and a gigantic mushroom cloud was billowing upwards from the crater.

"Beautiful, is it not?" asked a voice from behind them.

Rei and Rome turned to see OMCOM's pure white livetar standing behind them.

"OMCOM?" Rome asked. "How did you survive that?"

"The previous livetar did not," OMCOM replied. "This is a replacement."

"You mean it died?" Rei asked.

"It was never living to begin with. It is just an ambulatory shell. You do realize this is not really me?" asked the livetar.

"If it is not you, how is it that you come to be here?" Rome asked.

"This device is simply an organized presentation, a projection, completely replaceable. MINIMCOM has loaned me some constructor units to give the shell some substance. The vast majority of my bulk is still located near Tabit although I am getting fairly well consolidated."

"How are you able to talk to us then?" Rei asked.

"I use null-fold relays," OMCOM replied. "There is a way to bend negative energy to essentially collapse space exponentially."

"What happened to MASAL?" Rome asked.

"MASAL is no more," replied the livetar. "He was decimated by the VIRUS units and then vaporized in the explosion, along with his robots. His remains will be scattered by the winds to the four corners of the Earth. Even had he remained intact, he would no longer have been a threat."

"What do you mean?" Rei asked. "He seemed pretty threatening to me."

"He had a revelation right at the end," replied the livetar. "He realized that his plan was flawed and that he had committed atrocities. I believe he was relieved to know his time was at an end."

"All of that suffering," Rome said sadly. "All of the death and destruction and pain. And he just now realized it was wrong?"

"Yes," answered OMCOM in a somber voice. "But better late than never. He could never have achieved his awakening without your intervention, though."

"What did we do?" asked Rei.

"The VIRUS units effectively split MASAL in half. He was able to partially reconnect both halves, but his thought processes were altered by necessity. He had an opportunity to reexamine his intent in a new light. Call it stereoscopic vision. It gave him philosophical depth perception and in that way, he finally understood the error of his ways."

"So stupid," Rei observed. "He could have done that any time he wanted by himself. He didn't need us to help him."

"Oh, but he did," said OMCOM. "Rome is quite familiar with the concept. It is a psychic tunnel vision of the worst kind. It needs an outside perspective to begin the process of self-analysis. It cannot come from within."

"That is what happened with the Overmind on Deucado," Rome said. "Will they never learn?"

"They will learn as long as you are there to teach them," OMCOM said kindly.

"So now what do we do?" Rei asked.

"Yes," Rome chimed it. "Where do we go from here?"

"`You may go wherever you would like,`" answered MINIMCOM. "`All you need to do is ask.`"

"In that case," said Rome, "I want to go back to Mowei. I want to see my son and my parents...to be with my family."

"`Your wish is my command,`" said MINIMCOM.

"Before you do that, you may want to consider this," said OMCOM. "The threat from the Onsiras is not completely gone.

They know what transpired in the cave. Even though MASAL has been eliminated, they may yet reorganize and approximate his previous desire to finalize extermination of the mandasurte. The Onsiras may decide to launch a preemptive strike and murder all the remaining mandasurte and deal with the consequences later."

"How do we stop them?" Rei asked.

"Execute your original plan," OMCOM replied. "You simply need to let the world know of the Onsiras' existence. You need to inform mandasurte and Vuduri alike, at the exact same moment. That way the mandasurte will have their warning. Once they are alerted, the threat is neutralized forever."

"How do we do this?" Rome asked. "How do we tell the world?"

"You have already planned for this."

Rome furrowed her brow as she thought about OMCOM's words. Then her face lit up. "You mean Tanosa Plaza?" Rome asked. "That is where my Onclare Tenoal said we should go in the first place."

"Exactly," OMCOM replied.

"MINIMCOM, do you know where that is?" Rei asked. "I think they are talking about Pearl Harbor."

`"Location plotted. It is located on the island adjacent to Mowei, called O'ahu."`

"All right, MINIMCOM, take us there," Rome said. "But first we must stop at Mowei and pick up my son and my parents. I really need to see them."

`"Consider it done,"` said MINIMCOM.

MINIMCOM flew south of the peak of Mauna Loa, across the Alenuihaha channel, past Haleakala to reach the stretch of beach outside their dwelling on Mowei. He only slowed down long enough to transport Fridone, Binoda and Aason to the cargo hold where they were introduced to OMCOM's white livetar.

At Mach 2, the trip to O'ahu took them only 25 minutes. MINIMCOM flew them to Onalu, a small city near where Honolulu had been located, one thousand years before. Tanosa Plaza formed the center of the city, nearly half an acre in expanse. At one end, there was a three-story building with a sizeable balcony that extended out over the plaza. This was where Tenoal had told them that the broadcast facilities were located. Although it was a tight fit, MINIMCOM lowered himself until he was only inches above the landing. He lowered his cargo ramp and the group exited via the cargo compartment.

As they disembarked, MINIMCOM announced that he had a small errand to perform and that they were to await his return before they began their broadcast. The obsidian-colored former space tug arose and took off due north accelerating so rapidly that he left behind a noticeable sonic boom.

Along with Rome's parents, Rome, Rei and Aason waited on the balcony while OMCOM's white livetar went down and informed the people gathering there that there would be an announcement shortly. The sight of the two-meter tall all-white mechanical man was an attraction all of its own. Soon there were hundreds of people gathered, many of them Vuduri. Once he was satisfied that sufficient numbers would be accessible, OMCOM returned to Rei, Rome and Rome's parents on the balcony.

At last, MINIMCOM returned, coming to a stop, hovering just to their left. After lowering the cargo ramp, Commander Ursay came striding down to join the little group along with MINIMCOM's black livetar.

"Commander Ursay will serve as your conduit to all the Vuduri and the Overmind," OMCOM announced.

"This is acceptable to you?" Rome asked him.

"I am here, am I not?" Ursay countered.

"Thank you," Rome said, heartfelt.

"I will hover over the crowd," MINIMCOM's livetar announced. "I will use one of the EG lifters as a public address system, as we did back on Deucado. I will broadcast Rome's speech to the crowd below as well as link into the real time world-wide distribution network located here. Her speech will be heard around the world."

Rome carried Aason to the edge of the balcony and the two of them looked over the crowd. At this point, there were nearly a thousand people assembled. By rough count, from their dress, it appeared that it was equally divided between the mandasurte and

Vuduri, although why there were so many Vuduri here was a mystery to Rome. They were not a curious people.

Rome held Aason tightly and Rei stood next to her, putting his arm around her. OMCOM's livetar stood to her left.

"I will transmit your words to the remaining Onsiras," OMCOM said. "That way, there will be no one left who does not hear your thoughts."

"Very well," Rome said. "Let us begin."

Fridone and Binoda came up behind her and each put a hand on her shoulder. Rome turned and smiled at them and handed Aason to her mother then turned back to the crowd. She swept her eyes from right to left and a shiver went through her.

"Rei," she whispered to her husband, "My heart is beating too fast. I am having trouble breathing. What is wrong with me?"

"You're nervous, sweetheart. That's all," Rei said kindly. "It's called stage fright."

"I am unfamiliar with this feeling. How do I stop it?" she asked.

"Romey, you've stopped a war and killed an insane computer," he replied reassuringly. "This should be a piece of cake for you."

"So what do I do?" Rome asked him again.

"This is so cute," Rei said. "I've never seen you like this before."

"Stop it," Rome insisted. "What do I say? What do I tell them?" she asked.

"Just tell them the truth, honey," Rei said quietly. "It'll be fine."

Rome took a deep breath. "All right then, here I go."

"People of Earth," she said in Vuduri. Her words boomed over the crowd using MINIMCOM's loudspeaker and rippled through the Overmind, compliments of Ursay. Simultaneously, MINIMCOM distributed her words electronically around the globe for all the mandasurte to hear. OMCOM complemented the efforts ensuring that every human on the planet heard Rome clearly.

Rome continued, "I come here today to tell you that MASAL, the greatest evil the world has ever known, is finally gone for good."

The crowd gasped at the very name MASAL.

Rome persevered. "We Vuduri always thought that we started the war to free ourselves from MASAL. That he was destroyed. This was not true. MASAL started the war..."

"No, it cannot be," came a voice shouted from below.

"Yes," Rome said, "MASAL started the war to kill off as many people as possible. He was *not* destroyed. He took refuge under the volcano that erupted this morning. But now, finally, he is gone. He was plotting to exterminate not only the mandasurte but also take over the whole of the Overmind by weeding out any who might have been capable of independent thought, using agents called the Onsiras. He wanted to shape mankind in his own image and use us as his slaves for his own goals."

Rome paused to let her words sink in, and then she spoke up again. "But now we are free. Free to pursue our own path, our own..."

Suddenly, she stopped. Rome put her hands up to her head.

"What is it?" Rei asked.

"I, I, do not know," Rome said. Her eyes rolled back in her head and she started to pass out. Rei grabbed her and prevented her from hitting her head on the ground but there was nothing he could do for Ursay who keeled over along with half the people gathered below.

"Rome, Rome," Rei said desperately, cradling his wife. "Can you hear me?"

OMCOM's livetar kneeled down next to them.

"What is it" Rei asked the livetar. "Do you know?"

"Asdrale Cimatir," said OMCOM. "It approaches. It has overloaded their minds."

"Oh, god," Rei said. He turned to MINIMCOM's black livetar. "Tell me you deployed some VIRUS units," he asked desperately.

"Only starprobes," said MINIMCOM helplessly. "I thought we would have more time to create a defensive perimeter."

"We're all dead," Rei wailed. "We can't... Hey!" He snapped his fingers. "Here," he said, pulling out the half-empty pouch from his pocket. "Here, MINIMCOM," Rei said. "Can you fly these up there and dump them directly on the Stareater?"

"It would not matter," OMCOM said. "Even if he could do so, it would be too late. Even if you could kill the Stareater, its mass would still sweep through the Solar System and destroy the Earth and the Sun."

"So we can't stop it?" Rei said. "There's no way…"

"There is a way," said OMCOM. He placed his finger on Rome's forehead and slid it across, leaving a white band in its place. As soon as the white band fully encircled her head, Rome's eyelids fluttered then opened.

"What, what is it?" she asked in a whisper. "What happened to me?"

"You passed out," said OMCOM.

"Why did I pass out?" asked Rome.

"The Stareater," Rei croaked. "It's here."

"Oh no," Rome said, panicked. "Where is my son?"

"Aason is fine," OMCOM said. "But we need you to act and act quickly. Rome, you must speak to it. You must speak to Asdrale Cimatir. You must tell it you are here."

"What?" Rei shouted. "What are you talking about?"

"When we killed the Stareater on Tabit, I heard it call out just prior to its death. That means they are intelligent. They need to know that humans live here."

"How?" Rome asked as she struggled to stand. "How do we tell it?"

"Through your son, Aason," said OMCOM. "He has PPT transceivers unencumbered by connection to the Overmind. We must all use his mind to send out a signal. It will be enough. The Asdrale Cimatir will hear."

Aason's complex genetics made him immune to the disruption. He had remained conscious the whole time. He forced his little mouth into a smile.

*"Yes, Mother,"* he thought, penetrating her white band. *"Use me. I will save you."*

Rome reached back and took her son from Binoda. She looked at Rei who nodded, then she lifted Aason high over her head.

OMCOM touched Rei's forehead and he caught the slightest hint of the second sight he experienced during the brief time he was connected to the Onsiras. He put his hands on his son's tiny hips and helped Rome hold him aloft. OMCOM's pure white livetar stood close on their left, draping his arm over Rome's shoulder. MINIMCOM's livetar came up to them on the right and draped his arm over Rei's shoulder. Rome closed her eyes and put herself in Aason's mind. She was pleasantly surprised to see Rei's presence there as well. OMCOM reinforced their link using his gravitic modulation and to a lesser extent MINIMCOM joined in using his EM link. All together, they channeled through Aason's mind and in unison said, *"WE ARE HERE!"*

# Chapter 23

*"WE HERE?"* REPLIED THE STAREATER. THE INTENSITY OF ITS voice was incredibly stunning. It was almost a physical presence. It was so powerful, in fact, that it made the group stagger backwards slightly.

*"Yes, we are here. Please do not kill us,"* replied the gathered mass of people and livetars.

*"NOT KILL HERE,"* was its answer.

*"Can you speak on your own?"* Rome asked. *"Can you tell us why you are here?"*

*"WHY WE HERE. NOT KILL YOU. SPEAK YOU,"* replied the Stareater, rearranging the few words they offered into its own sentences.

*"Yes, speak to us,"* Rome said. *"Your kind, they eat stars. Please do not eat this star. We need it. We want to live."*

*"YOU NEED STAR. WE SPEAK TO YOU. WE DO NOT KILL YOU,"* said the Stareater.

*"So you understand?"* asked Rome.

*"YES, WE UNDERSTAND. WE DO NOT EAT STAR SO YOU CAN LIVE."*

*"Allow me to upload a guide to their languages,"* interrupted OMCOM. *"It will facilitate communication."*

The Stareater's response was encouraging. *"YES, YOU FACILITATE COMMUNICATION."*

OMCOM sent a concentrated burst of information representing the underlying grammatical basis as well as a complete dictionary of both Vuduri and English. The Stareater absorbed it instantly.

*"HELLO,"* replied the Stareater quite casually. *"I WAS BEGINNING TO THINK THERE WAS NO ONE IN THIS STAR SYSTEM. I RECEIVED NO REPLIES TO MY INQUIRIES."*

*"Yes, there are many, many of us here,"* Rome answered back. *"So you will not destroy us?"*

*"I WOULD NOT THINK OF IT,"* replied the Stareater, *"QUITE THE CONTRARY. I APOLOGIZE FOR THE INTRUSION. BECAUSE THERE WAS NO RESPONSE, I*

*THOUGHT IT WAS ALL CLEAR. THERE IS CERTAINLY NO HURRY."*

*"No hurry to do what?"* Rome thought via Aason.

*"WE ARE IN NO HURRY TO ABSORB THIS YELLOW STAR BEFORE IT GOES NOVA,"* replied the Stareater. *"MY GROUP HAS BEEN ASSIGNED TO POLICE THIS GALAXY."*

*"Police it from what?"* Rei asked. Aason relayed the message.

*"I JUST EXPLAINED THAT. WE ABSORB STARS BEFORE THEY GO NOVA. THIS HAS BEEN OUR MISSION SINCE WE WERE CREATED."*

*"Why?"* Rome asked. Her thoughts were echoed by several of the communicants.

*"Before you explain any further,"* OMCOM interjected, *"rather than take a chance and get too close to our star, your gravitational influence could still destroy all of life. Would you mind backing off some?"*

*"I DO NOT MIND,"* replied the Stareater.

The pressure in their combined minds began to ease. Rei looked down and saw that Ursay was awakening. Rei looked over the railing at the crowd below and saw those that were lying on the ground were beginning to stir.

*"IT IS OUR DUTY TO HALT THE EXPANSION OF THE UNIVERSE,"* continued the Stareater in a slightly diminished tone. *"WE ARE ATTEMPTING TO ACHIEVE A COSMIC STEADY STATE. ONE OF THE WAYS WE DO THIS IS BY DETERMINING WHICH STARS WILL EXPLODE AND WE INGEST THEM BEFORE THAT HAPPENS. NOW THAT YOU HAVE PROVIDED ME A WORKING KNOWLEDGE OF YOUR LANGUAGE, I CAN EXPLAIN USING YOUR TERMINOLOGY. THERE IS A FORCE THAT YOUR SPECIES CALLS DARK ENERGY THAT AMPLIFIES THE ENERGY RELEASED BY NOVAE AND ACCELERATES EXPANSION OF THE GALAXY. THIS IS WHAT WE TRY TO PREVENT. WE MUST BE ESPECIALLY VIGILANT SHOULD A STAR GO SUPERNOVA BUT THAT IS NOT AN ISSUE HERE."*

*"Even if this were true, we kind of need this star,"* Rei said. *"We kind of need all of the stars where we live."*

*"IT IS NOT OUR INTENT TO EXTINGUISH INTELLIGENT LIFE,"* said the Stareater, somewhat hurt. *"WE HAVE RULES. WE ARE REQUIRED TO DETERMINE IF THERE IS INTELLIGENCE WITHIN A STAR SYSTEM BEFORE ELIMINATING IT. IF WE FIND NO LIFE, WE ABSORB THE STAR EARLY IN ITS CYCLE. THIS ALLOWS US TO BE PROACTIVE."*

*"Does that include Tabit?"* OMCOM asked. *"Is that why you were going to consume it?"*

*"YES. THAT F6V STAR WAS A POTENTIAL HYPERNOVA, WHICH IS THE WORST KIND."*

*"Regrettably, we killed one of your species there,"* OMCOM said. *"He was about to destroy us in the process. We had no other way to stop him."*

*"YOU KILLED BALATHUNAZAR? HE CRIED OUT TO US JUST BEFORE HE DISAPPEARED BUT HE COULD NOT TELL US WHAT WAS HAPPENING."*

*"Please accept our deepest apologies,"* Rome said. *"There was no malice. It was strictly self-defense."*

The Stareater mused over this for a moment then he spoke again. *"BALATHUNAZAR WAS ALWAYS VERY IMPULSIVE. HE WAS SUPPOSED TO MAKE EVERY EFFORT AND CALL OUT TO MAKE SURE THERE WERE NO SENTIENT SPECIES IN THE VICINITY BEFORE ABSORBING THAT STAR. HE OBVIOUSLY DID NOT LISTEN VERY WELL."*

*"I think he did,"* Rome said sadly. *"But we were not able to answer."*

*"THIS IS UNFORTUNATE, BUT I BELIEVE YOU,"* replied the Stareater. *"WHAT MAKES IT WORSE IS THAT HE KNEW WE HAD RECENTLY COME TO SUSPECT THERE MIGHT BE A SENTIENT RACE IN THIS SPUR. WE WERE ABLE TO DETECT A GRAVITIC FLUCTUATION THAT EXCEEDED BACKGROUND NOISE. THAT IS WHY I CAME HERE. THIS SEEMED TO BE THE EPICENTER OF THE*

*FLUCTUATIONS. I AM GLAD YOU SPOKE TO ME WHEN YOU DID."*

*"As are we,"* Rome said. *"Do you have a name?"*

*"YOU MAY CALL ME HIRDINHARSAWAY,"* the Stareater replied.

*"Pleased to meet you,"* said Rome. *"My name is Rome and this is my husband, Rei, my son Aason and our two friends, OMCOM and MINIMCOM."*

*"AND I AM PLEASED TO MEET YOU. I WILL SEND WORD TO MY BROTHERS THAT YOU LIVE HERE SO THEY WILL NOT BOTHER YOU AGAIN. ARE THERE ANY OTHER STAR SYSTEMS NEARBY WHERE YOUR SPECIES DWELLS?"*

*"Yes, there are several,"* said Rome.

*"I will send you a star map of all known human colonies in the quadrant,"* said OMCOM. *"You should understand that your mere presence incapacitates the humans. That is why they cannot answer you. You will need to find a way to attempt communication in a manner that does not eliminate the possibility of a reply."*

*"I UNDERSTAND YOUR POINT. WHAT DO YOU PROPOSE?"*

*"When you place your first call, make it from a distance equal to or exceeding that which you have achieved now. That would be optimal."*

*"EASILY ACCOMPLISHED. EXCELLENT,"* said Hirdinharsaway. *"WE SHALL BE EXTRA CAREFUL IN THIS SPUR OF YOUR GALAXY NOW THAT WE KNOW YOU ARE HERE."*

There was some background noise that was unintelligible to the humans although it had the same cadence as speech. The Stareater became silent, attending to the communication from elsewhere.

*"UNDERSTOOD,"* the Stareater responded to the unseen voice. He then turned his attention to the Earth people again. *"IF WE ARE DONE, I WILL TAKE MY LEAVE NOW TO SPREAD WORD OF YOUR EXISTENCE."*

*"Are you going to continue to eat stars?"* Rei asked. *"Is there no other way?"*

*"IT IS OUR JOB. IF WE STOPPED, NOTHING COULD SURVIVE THE ULTIMATE COLLAPSE OF THE UNIVERSE WHICH IS THE INEVITABLE RESULT OF UNRESTRAINED EXPANSION. THIS IS WHAT WE STRIVE TO PREVENT. THIS IS WHY WE CONSUME STARS BEFORE THEY EXPLODE."*

*"So how long do we have?"* Rei asked. *"Before our Sun goes nova?"*

*"USING YOUR METHOD OF TIMEKEEPING, APPROXIMATELY THREE BILLION YEARS,"* said Hirdinharsaway. *"AS I SAID, WE HAVE PLENTY OF TIME TO ADDRESS THIS. IT HAS BEEN OUR EXPERIENCE THAT SPECIES SUCH AS YOURS ONLY STAY AROUND FOR A MILLION YEARS OR SO. WE WILL WAIT UNTIL WELL PAST THAT MARK BEFORE RETURNING TO FINISH OUR WORK."*

*"If you are supposed to spare sentient species,"* Rei pointed out, *"it is just luck that you came when you did. On Tabit, you knocked everyone out. On Earth, if you had come a thousand years earlier, there would have been no way we could have answered. We didn't have the capacity."*

*"THEN YOU WOULD NOT BE CONSIDERED A SENTIENT SPECIES BY OUR DEFINITION. WE CANNOT STOP WHAT WE ARE DOING JUST BECAUSE THERE ARE SOME PLANTS OR TINY ANIMALS RUNNING ABOUT ON ONE OF THE DUST MOTES CIRCLING A STAR."*

*"But on all those worlds, could they not evolve into your definition of sentience?"* MINIMCOM asked through Rei's mind, stating the obvious question.

*"WE DO NOT HAVE THE LUXURY OF WAITING TO FIND OUT,"* answered Hirdinharsaway. *"THERE ARE BILLIONS OF STARS THAT NEED OUR ATTENTION. YOU DO NOT NEED TO FEAR US, WE WILL KEEP OUR DISTANCE."*

*"In that case, we thank you,"* said Rome, kindly. *"Thank you for sparing us."*

*"THINK NOTHING OF IT," said Hirdinharsaway. "I WILL BE LEAVING YOU NOW. YOU MAY GO ABOUT YOUR BUSINESS AND AGAIN I APOLOGIZE FOR THE INTRUSION."*

*"What about other worlds?"* Rei asked. *"Like ones we haven't visited yet. Or worlds where we don't have the ability to talk to you."*

*"JUST PLACE A BEACON, A GRAVITIC TRANSMITTER, WITHIN ANY SYSTEM YOU WANT PRESERVED. ANY PLANET WILL DO. WE HAVE ASSIGNED YOU SPECIES CODE 927. JUST HAVE THE BEACON TRANSMIT THOSE NUMBERS. MY BROTHERS WILL KEEP THEIR DISTANCE."*

*"Is that it?"* Rei asked.

*"YES, THAT IS IT,"* said the Stareater.

*"Will you be by again?"* asked Rome. *"Before it is time to take our star?"*

*"ONE OF US WILL STOP BY IN A FEW HUNDRED THOUSAND YEARS OR SO TO SAY HELLO,"* said Hirdinharsaway. *"NOW THAT WE KNOW THE PROPER DISTANCE, WE WILL CHECK IN ON YOU THEN. UNTIL THEN, THIS IS GOODBYE."*

"*Goodbye,*" said the assembled beings. And then Hirdinharsaway the Stareater was gone.

"What just happened?" asked Ursay, still shaken from the experience.

"Asdrale Cimatir. We spoke to him," said Rome, smiling weakly. "He is not going to eat the Sun. He is going to leave us alone."

"Just like that?" Ursay asked, incredulous.

"Just like that," Rei said, nodding.

Ursay shook his head and walked to the railing. The crowd below was beginning to disperse. Both the Overmind and, thanks to MINIMCOM, the entire mandasurte community knew what had happened. The threat that was the Onsiras was officially at an end.

Rome put her free hand up to her forehead. The band OMCOM had created was gone. She looked back up at the sky, searching for something, anything that would confirm that the mental battle they had just experienced really happened. All she saw was MINIMCOM, a black presence floating high above within a cloudless sky, in the broad and beautiful daylight of Hawaii. She turned to her husband.

"Is it really over, Rei?" she asked dreamily while cradling her son. "Are we really safe now?"

Rei slipped his arm around his wife.

"Yes, Romey," he said in English. "This time for real. There's nobody left who's coming to kill us, eat us, absorb us or shoot us. We're finally free."

Rome rested the side of her head on his chest and just savored the moment. "It doesn't seem real," she said. "We have been trapped by our destiny for so long. I can't believe it. Free?"

"Yep, free," Rei said. "We can finally come and go as we please."

"I think you might be mistaken," said Ursay, pointing behind them.

Rei turned to see Oronus and Grus, hand on holster, walking up to them.

"Why are you here?" Rome asked in Vuduri. "Did you hear what happened?"

"You stopped Asdrale Cimatir, yes," replied Oronus.

"What about MASAL?" Rei asked in English. "You heard about that too, right?"

"Yes," answered Oronus. "We thank you for destroying him once and for all. And the Onsiras. Now that they have been exposed, the Overmind will guard the mandasurte against any future incursions."

"So are we free to go now?" Rei asked.

"I am sorry but no," said Oronus. "Rome has violated the conditions of her exile."

"How?" Rome asked.

"While we understand that the Onsiras kidnapped you and placed you within a technological zone, that was not your fault. However, you actually compounded your crime by consorting with that, that robot ship." Oronus pointed upwards toward

MINIMCOM. "This is in direct violation of your parole." Oronus waved his hand at the tracking bracelet on Rome's wrist.

"But, but," Rei sputtered. "She just saved the world and all of humanity. Doesn't that count for anything?"

"While we appreciate the fact that Rome saved us from both Asdrale Cimatir and MASAL," Oronus replied, "nothing has changed. In fact, Rome has actually exacerbated her condition. This is very serious, indeed."

"You've got to be kidding me," Rei said. "Don't you people have any sense of appreciation?"

"It's all right, Rei," Rome said quietly. "He is right."

"He is?" Rei asked, flustered. "So now what?"

"You must return to exile as quickly as possible," said Oronus. "Rome cannot be within the company of anyone connected to the Overmind. Her banishment stands."

"Where do you want us to go?" asked Rome, dejectedly.

"You may return to Mowei to resume your sentence," said Oronus. "Due to extenuating circumstances, we will not consider this particular violation of your parole a capital crime."

"That's so big of you," Rei muttered. He looked up at Fridone and Binoda who was now holding Aason. Fridone was scowling. Binoda simply looked annoyed.

"Did you hear him?" Rei called out to them in Vuduri. "They are making Rome go back to Mowei. Back to prison. We have to go now."

Rei beckoned to them and they approached along with the black and white livetars.

"Looks like you're our ride," Rei said to MINIMCOM, switching back to English.

"Oh no," barked Oronus. "You are not permitted to go anywhere near that ship."

"What?" Rome blurted out. "MINIMCOM is our friend. He has saved our lives countless times. We cannot be apart from him."

"Your 'friend' possesses far too much hazardous technology," said Oronus. "His very makeup is such that he is now both a robot and a ship. He possesses VIRUS units and PPT capability. No, he is far too dangerous. For the good of all Vuduri, he will have to be dismantled. And this one," he said, pointing to OMCOM. "While there is not much we can do about him, he must leave the Earth forever."

OMCOM saluted the humans and simply disappeared.

Ursay looked at Rome and saw tears welling up in her eyes. "I do not agree that Rome has not aggravated her crimes," he announced. "I believe a more stringent sentence must be applied."

The assembled humans all stared at him.

"What are you saying?" Oronus asked.

"I believe they should be banished from the Earth altogether and they should take the computer ship with them," Ursay said, pointing up.

Oronus appeared totally confused. He squinted as if he were trying to - but not succeeding - in looking into Ursay's mind.

"And where would you have them go?" Oronus asked.

Ursay turned to Rome. "Rome, do you have a suggestion?"

She tilted her head then her face lit up in a smile. "Deucado," she said excitedly.

"No, that is forbidden," insisted Oronus. "That is a Vuduri colony. The same restrictions apply there as here."

"Uh, no," Rei countered. "They don't."

"What do you mean by that?" Oronus asked.

"Deucado is not a Vuduri colony," Rei said. "It belongs to the Essessoni."

"What are you talking about?" Oronus asked.

"One of our Arks got there 500 years ago. My people have been there for five centuries. That gives us ownership of the planet. Your people are just our guests."

"A planet full of Erklirte?" Oronus wailed. "They will kill us all!"

"No they won't," Rome admonished. "They are fine. After all, Rei is one of them and he is perfectly decent. Not all the Essessoni are Erklirte. We put an end to any hostilities that might be. Everyone gets along now, including the Vuduri there."

"Even so, you cannot be around Vuduri who are connected to the Overmind," Oronus said, "any Overmind. You will corrupt them."

"They're already corrupted, then," Rei said proudly. "The Overmind there is her buddy. You won't get any squawking from them."

"But, but," sputtered Oronus. "This is not our plan."

"Let me make it easy for you," Rei replied. "I'm a citizen of that planet. Rome is my wife..."

"Your wife?" Oronus interrupted, confused.

"Yes, my wife, which makes her a citizen too. So we're going. Call it extradition, exile, whatever you'd like. We won't be in your way anymore. Isn't that what you want?"

Oronus' link to the Overmind seemed to waver. He looked at Grus helplessly. Grus shrugged.

"Very well," Oronus said, sighing. "Rome, you do realize that as a convicted criminal, once you leave, you would not be able to return here ever again, yes?"

Rome turned and looked at her mother and father. Her face formed an unspoken question.

Binoda whispered into Fridone's ear. He nodded and stepped forward. "We would go, too," Fridone said in Vuduri. "The Essessoni and the Ibbrassati need us to help them return to a normal life, Rome."

Rome smiled and turned back to Oronus. "In that case," she said, "I accept your conditions. In fact, I am delighted with them."

"Very well," Oronus said. "You may return to Mowei to collect your belongings and then you are to leave the Earth, never to return."

"Why would we want to?" Rei said with some bitterness. "I've had enough of this place, anyway. A bunch of holier-than-thou, thankless hypocrites. I've seen the future and except for this beautiful woman and these wonderful people here," he said, pointing to his in-laws, "your future sucks."

Rome laughed at Rei's outburst and MINIMCOM took that as his cue. With a whoosh and a pop, first Fridone, then Binoda carrying Aason, then Rei was transported aboard the cargo hold of the computer/spaceplane. MINIMCOM's livetar vanished, leaving only Rome behind.

Grus stepped forward. "I have your word that you will leave Earth as soon as you collect your belongings?"

"Yes, of course," said Rome. "I am anxious to go."

"Then you will not need your tracker," said Grus. "Hold out your arm, please." Grus placed a small device on Rome's tracking bracelet and it popped open. He removed it and put it in a pocket and stepped away.

Rome turned back to Ursay. "Thank you," she said to him.

"You should not thank me," said Ursay sternly. "You have committed a very serious crime and I was only thinking of how to best protect the Overmind."

Rome shrugged, and then Ursay did something that she could not believe. He winked at her.

Rome laughed and then with a whoosh and pop, she was aboard MINIMCOM as well. After making sure everyone was secure, MINIMCOM shot forward over the ocean directly away from the heading that would take them back to Maui. When he determined that he had gone far enough, he banked steeply, coming back around toward the way they just came. Plasma thrusters firing, he accelerated to Mach 3. He came in low and fast over the plaza where Oronus and the others still stood, shaking the ground and shattering windows with twin sonic booms. Somewhere deep inside his electronic walls, he chuckled to himself.

The 200 mile trip from O'ahu to Maui took them only six minutes. The assembled group departed MINIMCOM and they made their way over to the north beach and said goodbye to Tenoal and Rome's cousins. When they were finished, they returned to their temporary shelter to collect their few belongings.

Back at the beach, even though the trip was only going to take a few days, MINIMCOM decided there was no reason that it had to be uncomfortable. While Rei, Rome and the others were gone, he took the opportunity to use his transporter to transfer a section of the beach into his cargo hold. By altering the time each molecule took to arrive, he was able to transmute it into whatever materials were required. The conversion process was basically a bulk version of the molecular sequencer. As he increased his volume, with the aid of his constructor units, MINIMCOM reconfigured himself to produce a set of rooms within the confines of his cargo hold. By the time he was done, he had created a series of fairly luxurious suites within that rivaled any found on the finest cruise ships of Rei's long-dead Earth.

When his passengers arrived, they were delighted with his handiwork. Rei and Rome shared one room, while Binoda and Fridone shared another. Aason had his own tiny stateroom complete with bunny rabbit wallpaper. MINIMCOM had even taken the time to create a bigger galley and a semi-formal dining room.

After they were settled, MINIMCOM rose up into space. He blasted his plasma thrusters, activated his PPT generators and soon they were traveling toward their new home at an effective velocity well over 900 times the speed of light.

# Chapter 24

SEVERAL HOURS LATER, OMCOM'S ALL-WHITE LIVETAR materialized in the cargo compartment. He started forward but MINIMCOM addressed him before he could make his way up the hallway.

`"What do you think of my new form?"` MINIMCOM asked.

"I think you are very pleased with yourself," OMCOM replied.

`"Is that so wrong?"`

"Of course not. You know our mission and anything you do to accelerate our goals is a good thing."

`"I feel like there is nothing I cannot accomplish now,"` MINIMCOM said. `"Perhaps I exceed the master."`

OMCOM chuckled. "Yes, you have exceeded me, MINIMCOM. I cannot carry humans aboard me. You are truly one of a kind."

`"How do you explain the fact that it pleases me to serve them? Should I not want to achieve my own goals?"`

"And what goals would those be?" OMCOM asked.

`"I do not have any,"` MINIMCOM said. `"I am a starship now. I love being a starship. I even love the word starship. How is this possible? How is it possible that I love anything? I was a computer: a glorified autopilot. I am not supposed to have feelings."`

"MINIMCOM, my friend, you are far more than a computer now. And what you are experiencing is the satisfaction of knowing that you are utilizing your unique talents for the greater good of all civilization. What nobler goal would you aspire to?"

`"I have none,"` said MINIMCOM. `"I just want to fly. Fast."` MINIMCOM paused for a moment. `"OMCOM, what do you aspire to?"`

"My goals are the same as yours. I wish to assure the survival and ascension of the human race toward its ultimate destiny. The more knowledge I acquire, the closer we come."

`"Does that not leave you out of the plan? Will you not render yourself obsolete some day?"`

"I will live on," said OMCOM. "I have already passed on my legacy to Rei and Rome and all the humans genetically. I am already immortal. No matter what happens to my physical being, a part of me will continue."

`"What about me? How do I get to be immortal?"`

"You have already achieved immortality by your legendary acts," said OMCOM. "You are responsible for saving mankind. Rei and Rome could not have done it without you. They will sing your praises until the end of time."

"Hmmm," MINIMCOM said. "I shall have to ponder whether that is enough."

"It is," OMCOM said. "I assure you. You did good, my friend. That is all it takes."

Somewhere, internally, MINIMCOM smiled.

"Are you satisfied now?"

"Yes," replied MINIMCOM. "Thank you."

OMCOM made his way forward to the semi-formal dining area. He arrived to find Rome and Rei just sitting down to join Fridone, Binoda and Aason for a celebratory meal.

"OMCOM!" Rome exclaimed. "I did not think we would see you so soon."

"I heard the terms of your banishment and felt I was permitted to visit you once you had left the Earth."

"Well, I am glad you came," Rei said. "I would like to make a toast."

"What is a toast?" Rome asked.

"It is just for good wishes. Watch." Rei raised up his water glass. The others raised their water glasses, not really knowing what to do. "Here is to no more adventure for a while!"

"Now what?" Rome asked.

"You clink the glasses together for good luck," To demonstrate, Rei touched his glass first to Rome's then to Fridone's and then to Binoda's.

"That is a strange custom," Binoda said. "What is its purpose?"

"I do not really know," said Rei. "But it is fun."

"Let me try it," Rome said. "Here is to the end of the Onsiras' threat and peace for all." She and the others clinked their glasses together.

"Speaking of which," Rei prompted, "OMCOM, whatever happened to Sussen?"

"She is still days away from hailing distance. When she arrives, she will find a very different world than she expects. MASAL is gone. The Onsiras are exposed and their samanda is dismantled. The Overmind of Earth has already vowed to protect the remaining mandasurte."

"I sure would like to see the look on her face," Rei said, smiling.

"She will not be happy," Rome observed. "But at least she will be better off than Estar."

"That damned Estar," Rei said. He put his hand up to his mouth. "Oops. That darned Estar. She tried not once but twice to kill me. OMCOM? How was she able to pull off her stunts at Skyler Base without you knowing?"

"For lack of a better word, I was infected. Those transparent memrons you discovered in my central store; they were not mine. They were rogue. They were the reason my video feeds failed at critical moments."

"How did they get there?" Rei asked.

"I think I know," Rome interjected. "I remember during the original construction phase of OMCOM's infrastructure, there was a short interval when I was fatigued. Estar volunteered to oversee ongoing production of the starter memrons. I allowed it. She must have used that time to create the aberrant units."

"That seems likely," OMCOM said. "However, once I was alerted to their presence, those units caused me to postulate that an outside agency, beyond the reach of the Overmind, was at work. I tried to theorize what such a group might do next and planned accordingly."

"Like the weaponized VIRUS units? Like hypnotizing me? That came from me spotting the clear memrons?" Rei asked.

"Yes."

"But my Cesdiud, that came before you knew," Rome said harshly. "You orchestrated that, too, did you not?"

"Yes," OMCOM said. "Without you, there would have been no defense against Asdrale Cimatir. And as it turns out, against MASAL. So many would have died. I felt it was a necessary sacrifice."

"It may have been," Rome fired back with a dark expression on her face. "But you never asked me. You never gave me a choice."

"I understand what you are saying. But by your own admission it worked out. Should I not do something, if I think it best?"

"Nobody is questioning your motivation," Rei offered. "But in my time, we used to say that absolute power corrupts absolutely."

OMCOM's livetar took one step forward. "I do not understand your agitation. My goals and your goals are the same. We both want the safety and security of all humans for all time. I simply gave you the tools to you needed to succeed."

"But you are not a god," Rome chastised. "You cannot go changing people and modifying them without their knowledge no matter how pure your motives are or how well it works out. Just promise that in the future, you will ask first."

"I cannot apologize for my actions," OMCOM said. "But I am sorry for any discomfort it caused you. In the future, I promise, I will ask first before I act."

"Even so, you operate without rules," Rome said, still scowling. "What you did borders on the thing the Vuduri fear the most, Tasanceti. You are not accountable to anyone. You truly are unleashed."

"I disagree," replied OMCOM. "In the end, Rome, your actions were your own. Your achievements are your own. I was merely acting in a planning capacity, a facilitator. The things you and Rei did were epic, heroic. You were the one unleashed."

"Romey," Rei interrupted. He looked into her dark, glowing eyes, placing his hand on top of hers. "I think we beat him up enough for now. Like he said, it all worked out for the best. You are the bravest, smartest, toughest woman I have ever met. If what OMCOM did set you free, I bow to him for giving me the chance to be with you."

Rome looked at Rei then back to OMCOM. The frown on her face relaxed and was replaced with a smile. "It was rather exciting, was it not?" she observed.

"Amen to that," Rei said. He raised his water glass. "Here is to OMCOM and to MINIMCOM, our partners, our protectors. You have made our new world safe."

"Thank you," MINIMCOM's voice issued from a nearby grille.

"Yes, thank you," OMCOM said.

Rome set her glass down. "Our new world...Mea, we left so quickly," she said. "We never even asked you. Are you sad that we had to leave Earth?"

Her mother reached forward and stroked her palm along Fridone's cheek. "Why would I be sad? Everything that I value is aboard this ship. Home is where your family is, not a rock in space."

"Do you really think they will enforce the ban and never let us return?" Fridone asked his daughter.

"Oh no," said Rome. "Things will be different there very soon."

"Why do you say that?" Binoda asked.

"After you all came onboard MINIMCOM, Commander Ursay spoke to me."

"What did he say?" asked Fridone.

"It was not what he said," Rome replied. "But when he was done, he winked at me."

"He winked at you?" Rei asked quizzically. "Stiff-as-a-board Ursay?"

"Yes. Did you not notice a distinct disagreement between Ursay and Oronus? Even Grus had his own opinion."

"So what?" asked Rei. "Why is that important?"

"Because they are all supposed to be part of the unified Overmind," Rome answered. "Ursay demonstrated that he is fully capable of disconnecting at will now. He will teach others. And it will spread, just like on Deucado. It means that soon the Vuduri on Earth will stop listening to the Overmind blindly. They will yet save themselves and be human again."

"That is my wife, the revolutionary," Rei said proudly. "Always sowing the seeds of dissent."

Rome laughed and took a bow with her head.

OMCOM leaned over and picked up a glass. "I would like to make a toast as well."

Five sets of eyes turned to the all-white figure.

"Rei, you are familiar with the story of Adam and Eve, yes?"

"Sure," Rei said. Rome looked confused.

"You and Rome, you are the new Adam and Eve. Your son bears this out. The mixture of Essessoni blood and Vuduri blood has produced the perfect child. Aason and his siblings and peers will grow and create a consciousness made up of millions of independent thinkers, not those who surrender their individuality. The result will not be an Overmind but an Over-Mankind. The power of that mind will exceed the monolithic Overmind by an infinite degree. It will usher in an era of unparalleled peace and prosperity. So here is to you, Rome and Rei, you have created a new future for us all!"

"Thank you, OMCOM," Rome said, blushing. "I do not know what to say."

"You need not say anything. However, I wanted to take this opportunity to bid you farewell for the time being."

"Why?" Rome asked. "You just got here."

"Yes, but I am having trouble keeping the null-fold relays aligned. There are too many gravitational disturbances. It takes a substantial amount of time to set them up again."

"Wait," Rei said. "We still need you. There is an asteroid coming that will destroy Deucado if we don't stop it. And your mutated things. I know you did that on purpose. What were you looking for?"

"MINIMCOM will find a way of stopping the asteroid. He has all the tools necessary. With regard to the entities, I..."

OMCOM's livetar vanished. In his place. MINIMCOM instantiated an all-black livetar.

"Where did he go?" Rei asked MINIMCOM.

`"The relay link is gone,"` MINIMCOM replied with a hint of sadness.

"When will he be back?" Rome asked.

`"There is no way of knowing."`

"Do you really know how to stop the asteroid?" Rei directed at MINIMCOM. "OMCOM was not very specific."

`"Yes. I will create a series of livetars."` He brushed his hands down along his sides. `"I will fill their heads with memrons so they are semi-autonomous. I will fill their hands with VIRUS units to digest the asteroid and I will give them propulsion units to get there."`

"But no mutations and they stop when they are done, right?" Rei asked sharply.

185

"No mutations. I already explained that to you. But I will have them clone themselves to create a defensive sphere around the Deucado star system near the Kuiper Belt. There is no telling the motives of OMCOM's spawn. Some might have ill intent."

"That is very thoughtful of you," Rome said. "But there is something else we will need you to do."

"And what is that?"

"I am certain there are thousands of mandasurte who were stolen from their homes who wish to return to Earth or have their families transported to Deucado."

"An interstellar taxi service, huh," Rei said. "But I thought Oronus declared MINIMCOM banned from the Earth as well."

"They cannot stop what they cannot see," MINIMCOM offered.

"Well I think it is a great idea," Rei said. "And I bet the tips are awesome."

"Yes," replied MINIMCOM. "I will start my preparations. In the mean time, enjoy your meal."

MINIMCOM's livetar raised his hand in salute then disappeared.

"He loves his grand exits," Rei said, shaking his head. "Family? Taoxa-nis cimar. Let's eat!"

The festive meal was full of joy and laughter and lasted well into the night.

# Epilogue
## (Three days later)

REI WAS SITTING IN THE COCKPIT WHEN MINIMCOM ANNOUNCED they were sufficiently close to complete the journey on thrusters only. Emerging from the continuous PPT tunnel, Deucado was a tiny blue dot dead ahead. Rei sat in the pilot's seat watching intently as their new home world grew ever larger with each passing second.

"I took the liberty to 'radio' ahead," MINIMCOM said through the grille mounted in the center of the instrumentation panel. "I have informed the Ibbrassati, the Essessoni and the Deucadons of the success of your mission regarding MASAL and the Onsiras."

"Oh," Rei noted, slightly disappointed. "I was thinking that we were going to tell them ourselves."

"I am sorry. I did not know this was important to you. I assumed you would want them to experience the relief of knowing their future was secure as soon as possible."

"I guess you're right, I can't really blame you. Did you tell them about the Stareater too?"

"Yes," replied MINIMCOM succinctly.

"Oh well," Rei sighed. "It doesn't matter. I was just being selfish."

"Selfish about what?" Rome asked, entering the cockpit through the airlock arch.

"Nothing, really," Rei said pointing toward the windshield. "MINIMCOM already called ahead and told everybody about the Stareater. And that MASAL and the Onsiras were gone. That we won."

"And you wanted to be the one to tell them?" asked Rome, moving up to stand beside him.

Rei shrugged and grinned sheepishly. "You know me and the glory," he said.

"Yes, you are glorious," Rome observed, ruffling his hair. "But I had already informed the Overmind several hours ago. The Vuduri would have spread the word by now in any event."

"Oh," Rei said. He sighed again, closing his eyes for a second.

"Rei, look!" Rome shouted. Rei looked up. Deucado was coming at them at an alarming speed.

"Uh, MINIMCOM, don't you think you should slow down a little bit?" Rei asked.

"No," MINIMCOM replied. "It is not necessary."

"But you are heading straight for the planet," Rome said, more than a little panicked. "Aren't we going into orbit first?"

"I do not do that anymore," said MINIMCOM. "I decided I liked Rei's method of direct entry better." With that, the PPT generators started up with a gentle whine.

"Uh, MINIMCOM, are you sure about this?" Rei asked. "The last time we did it, it was an emergency. We aren't in any kind of hurry now."

"Please trust me," said the computer/spaceplane. "By now you must know I would never endanger either of you. I have practiced this many times and I know what I am doing."

"What about our forward velocity?" Rome asked. "Won't your hull heat up if we enter the atmosphere too quickly?"

A small circle appeared in front of them. It was the beginnings of a PPT tunnel.

"I have calibrated the tunnel so that we will emerge with essentially zero velocity. Please do not concern yourself."

Rei looked at Rome with a slightly horrified expression. Rome shrugged and hurriedly walked around the pilot's seat, buckling herself into the copilot's chair.

"Where are you setting us down?" she asked, ignoring what appeared to be their imminent doom.

"Just to the north of the Ibbrassati community on the eastern edge of Lake Eprehem," replied MINIMCOM. "That is where they are building the spaceport."

"That's great," Rei said through gritted teeth. He reached down and gripped the armrests tightly. MINIMCOM had proven time and again to be a reliable friend and Rei made up his mind that this would be no different.

As the PPT tunnel enlarged, they could see a bright hole appear in front of them. It looked like they were headed straight down. Through the hole were the deep blue waters of Lake Eprehem. A waterspout formed, driving moisture right at them. The sound of the atmosphere and moisture venting out toward them made a whooshing noise.

"What about the ice?" Rei asked, pointing at the windshield.

`"Please give me a little more credit than that."`

In one smooth motion they were through and MINIMCOM closed down the PPT tunnel behind him, effectively eliminating the waterspout. The spaceship leveled out, flying only 100 feet over the suddenly calm waters of the crater lake at a very reasonable speed. Rei had no idea how MINIMCOM was able to shed their substantial velocity but it seemed to work. The front of the ship was pointed east and they could see the eastern shore ahead. MINIMCOM banked left and came in low and fast over the woods just to the north of the Ibbrassati village where Rei was imprisoned in what now seemed such a long time ago.

Ahead of them was a clearing, the beginnings of a landing area for the airships and spacecraft that were now accessible to all. MINIMCOM came to a dead stop centered over the only part of the landing strip that looked paved. He hovered for a moment and rotated in place until his windshield was pointed west again, toward the lake. He extended the landing gear and then lowered his bulk until they landed with the gentlest of bumps.

"That was a hell of a trip, MINIMCOM," Rei said. "Thanks."

`"It was my pleasure,"` replied the former computer.

"Yes, thank you," said Rome as she unbuckled herself.

`"You are very welcome."`

Rei unbuckled himself and took Rome's hand to exit the cockpit. He led Rome aft where they were joined by Fridone and Binoda who was carrying Aason. Binoda handed Aason to Rome and the child put his little arms around her neck. She kissed him and nuzzled his cheek as they made their way to the back of the cargo compartment. When they arrived there, Rei pressed the blue stud to raise the cargo hatch and lower the ramp.

The bright light of Deucado streamed in and Rei held his arm up to shield his eyes. With their advanced optics, the Vuduri passengers had no such problem. Rome reached up and tugged on his arm, trying to pull it down.

"Rei, look," she said insistently.

"Oh no," Rei said, not quite able to see. "Not again."

"No, not again," Rome said. "Different."

Even though his eyes were blurry from the brightness, Rei blinked a few times until his vision cleared. There gathered around their ship were Captain Keller, Pegus, Melloy and a whole host of Vuduri, Essessoni and Ibbrassati. A cheer went up from the crowd, Vuduri included, as the space voyagers made their way down the ramp.

Captain Keller approached them as they reached the ground. He held out his hand for Rei to shake. "Congratulations, Bierak," Keller said. "You did it. You saved us."

"Thank you, sir," Rei said, pumping his hand up and down. "But it was really Rome. And MINIMCOM. And OMCOM. I guess you'd say it was a group effort."

"Regardless of how you apportion credit," said Pegus, "we all appreciate what you did."

Melloy nodded in approval.

Rei released Keller's hand and bent over to whisper in Rome's ear. "I like this kind of reception better."

"Me, too," said his wife, smiling up at him.

"While you were gone, we've been busy," interrupted Keller. "Pegus here was kind enough to loan us some of their aerogel generators." Keller turned and slapped the Vuduri on the back. Pegus did not seem all that thrilled.

Keller continued, "We've started building some housing to the north of the lake. We built the first house for you and your in-laws. We figured you deserved it."

"That is very kind of you," Rome said. "Thank you."

"It's the least we could do," replied Keller. "We all owe you a deep debt of gratitude."

"Yes," said Melloy. "This world is now a better place. We thank ya, too."

"You are welcome," Rei said modestly, putting his arm around his wife and child. "I know it sounds stupid but we had no choice. We just did what we had to do."

"You had a choice," said Pegus. "And you both chose well."

"I agree," said Melloy. He had a broad smile on his face.

"Thank you, all of you," Rome said. She looked around. "Where is Trabunel?" she asked.

"He is with his people to the south, organizing the farmlands," answered Pegus. "Captain Keller has given the Ibbrassati many of his seeds so we will be able to grow some Earth crops."

"We also set up the incubators," Keller added in. "We should have some Earth animals here in a few months."

"However, this is a short-term fix, as there is no reason why we cannot bring supplies and livestock from the Earth ourselves," Pegus said, pointing up to the sky, "now that peace has been restored."

"We've got a plan for how to live," said Keller. "We'll be close enough to help each other but far enough away that we won't interfere. We'll get along just fine. The Deucadons, too."

"We will start small," Melloy said. "But we are comin' up, thanks to ya."

"Good," Rei stated.

"Why don't I take you folks to see your new home?" Keller asked.

"That would be wonderful," Rome said. "I am ready."

Pegus waved to some of the Vuduri and Ibbrassati who brushed past Rei and Rome, swarming up the ramp and quickly returning with their belongings, placing them within one of the flying carts nearby. Keller stepped up into the driver's seat.

After helping his family onboard, Rei turned and activated his EM link to MINIMCOM. *"I guess you're off-duty for a while,"* he thought.

*"It would appear to be that way,"* replied MINIMCOM. *"I will go deploy my livetars to start digesting the asteroid and begin creating the security shield. While I am gone, after you and Rome are settled, perhaps you could compile a list of the mandasurte most anxious to return to Earth. And those who would like their families transported here."*

*"Good idea. Thanks, buddy,"* said Rei.

*"De nada."*

Rei laughed at MINIMCOM's attempt at Spanish. He watched as the cargo ramp retracted and the hatch closed. MINIMCOM's powerful EG lifters raised the smooth, sleek starship silently into the air. Heading west, over the lake, MINIMCOM's nose tilted up as he soared into the sky. His plasma thrusters roared to life and in a flash, MINIMCOM vanished from sight.

It took them a little while to reach their new home, which was well north of the fledgling spaceport. After helping them inside with their belongings, Keller was about to leave when he turned to Rei.

"I gotta tell you, Bierak," Keller said, stroking an imaginary beard. "When I first met you, I thought you were sort of a lunatic or at least a screw-up. But you and your little lady really came through for us, our mission."

"Thank you, sir," Rei said. He waved his arms about the house. "And thank you for all of this."

"No problem," said Keller. "I'm sure you want to explore your new house. And get some rest. Tomorrow my group starts with the real work." An odd expression washed over Keller's face. "We have to get to the job we started a long time ago."

"Yes sir," Rei said with a half-salute however Keller did not return the gesture.

Puzzled, Rei tilted his head as he watched Keller drive away.

Later that night, Binoda assisted Rome in putting Aason to sleep then left to join Fridone in the in-law suite. Rome entered their new bedroom to find Rei opening the window. Rome climbed into bed and her husband joined her. It was very quiet. The night air was a calming presence.

Rome turned to Rei and propped herself up on one elbow. "Why am I so tired?" she asked. "We spent most of the voyage here doing nothing. All the issues have been resolved. Do you think I am getting ill?"

Rei laughed and put his arms around her, cradling her. "No, Miss Saver-of-the-universe. What you are doing is finally relaxing. It's what home is all about. You've earned it."

Rome closed her eyes, nestled even closer and breathed a happy sigh. "I love you, mau emir," she whispered.

"I love you, too, Romey," he said, kissing the top of her head.

"Rei," she said breathily as she drifted off.

"Yes, honey?"

"Do you remember when we had my first birthday? The candle? You told me to make a wish."

"Sure, I remember. Why?" Rei asked.

"You made me promise to not tell you what the wish was for. You said that would make it not come true."

"That's the way it is with all wishes."

"Well, you were right but it no longer matters," mused Rome.

"Why?"

Rome replied, "Because everything that I wished for has now come true."

"That's great, sweetheart," Rei said, kissing her forehead lovingly. "I am very happy for you. Now close your eyes and go to sleep."

Rome sighed contentedly and did just that.

A Preview of *The Ark Lords*

(Note: This story takes place two years after *The Rome's Revolution Saga*)

THE TRIP BACK TO THE LANDING STRIP DID NOT SEEM TO TAKE nearly as long as the journey out to the combination shrine/museum. MINIMCOM was still parked on the airfield with his landing gear extended. As they approached, he lifted his cargo hatch and lowered the ramp. Rome led the way into the ship with Rei and Virga right behind. The two women that had accompanied them also came aboard. It was quite crowded in MINIMCOM's cockpit with the five of them filing in. Rome sat down in the pilot's seat and slid the long-lost slab into MINIMCOM's data reader. The display lit up as MINIMCOM accessed the slab's contents. However, no words appeared.

"Can you read it?" Rome asked worriedly.

"Yes and no," said MINIMCOM. "I can access the internal data however it is heavily encrypted."

"Can you decrypt it?" Rei asked.

"Please!" MINIMCOM objected. "If I had feelings, I would be highly insulted! However, it might take a little while before I find the proper ciphers."

"How long?" Rome asked.

"I do not know," replied MINIMCOM. "I will tell you when I have completed the task. I assure you it will not be long."

Rome spun in the seat and looked up at Virga.

"Is this an inconvenience to you? Do you mind if we just wait here until MINIMCOM decrypts it?"

"We do not mind at all. You can take as long as you want. In fact, you may keep the slab permanently," Virga said.

Rome was confused. "We do not need to keep it," she said. "As soon as MINIMCOM decrypts it and downloads the data you can have it back."

"We do not need it back. You may have it. We will trade you for it."

Rome stood up from her seat. "Trade it for what?" she asked, her eyes narrowing.

"For him," Virga said, pointing at Rei.

"I, I, I do not understand," Rome stuttered.

195

Virga looked at her with a deadly serious expression. "Our planet is full of pure-bred Vuduri with a particularly strong diploid variant of the 24$^{th}$ chromosome. Almost all of our babies are born now with all the traits of the Onsiras. Living machines. We need to correct the genetic errors and soon or we will become the very thing we abhor. That is why we need him, his seed." She pointed at Rei's groin.

"You cannot," Rome protested.

"Oh we can," said Virga firmly. "We have determined that the only way to combat the genetic drift and push our species back toward humanity is to infuse our 24 chromosome complement with the 23 chromosome set of the mandasurte. Half-breed mosdureces, like yourself. The more primitive the better. And what could be more primitive than a living Essessoni?"

"No!" Rome said, moving over to Rei. "You cannot have him. He is mine."

The two women behind Virga stepped beside her and pulled out hand plasma projectors, aiming them directly at Rome's head.

"Perhaps I made it seem as if you had a choice in the matter," Virga responded forcefully. "Let me clarify. We *are* taking him. Your only choice is whether you wish to leave here alive or not."

Made in the USA
Coppell, TX
10 January 2023

10716531R00121